GW00793021

'Ruth, calm down, I never suspected you could be so emotional,' Dan murmured soothingly. 'I appreciate your special interest in my son. But you've seen for yourself that Ditchingham House really is a happy and caring school. You're already making a valuable contribution, but you must concede that I have much more experience of children than you do. Some seven-year-old boys do tend to be accident prone, especially if they're vigorous and healthy and highly active. But the answer isn't to wrap them in cotton wool. Believe me, I understand my son. I was just like him at that age—always in trouble, always hurting myself. And look at me, I've survived.'

'It's my job to concern myself with *all* the children's welfare. It is unfortunate but purely coincidental that Danny is *your* son. I'm convinced he would benefit from being a day boy and I would be shirking my responsibilities if I didn't tell you so, regardless of who you happen to be. If you ignore my professional advice, then that's entirely up to you. But don't accuse me of being emotional!'

Hospital romance must be second nature to Anna Ramsay, whose parents met when her mother was a ward sister and her father—not the doctor in this case—the hospital chaplain. Although she read history at university and taught for some years, Anna is now taking advantage of her own past experience of vacation jobs on hospital wards, and having a very up-to-the-minute source of information in her RGN nurse daughter.

Previous Titles

HEARTBEAT
ANGEL IN DISGUISE

ACCIDENT PRONE

BY

ANNA RAMSAY

MILLS & BOON LIMITED
ETON HOUSE   18-24 PARADISE ROAD
RICHMOND   SURREY   TW9 1SR

*First published in Great Britain 1989
by Mills & Boon Limited*

© Anna Ramsay 1989

*Australian copyright 1989
Philippine copyright 1989
This edition 1990*

ISBN 0 263 76693 4

*Set in Times 11 on 12 pt.
03 – 9001 – 51750*

Typeset in Great Britain by JCL Graphics, Bristol

Made and Printed in Great Britain

CHAPTER ONE

THE guard slammed the last carriage door shut, put his whistle to his lips . . .

Ruth dropped her change into her pocket, tucked her *Nursing Times* under her arm, flashed the man at the gate a glimpse of her ticket to Bath, took the steps at breakneck pace and charged down the platform.

This burst of energy was a bit of a miracle, considering she'd worked all night, skipped breakfast, and was en route for a job she wasn't desperate to get. But having got this far, elbows jammed into her sides in a smoking compartment all the way to Bristol, she was blowed if she was going to fall at the last hurdle. Sheer force of will was going to get her on the Bath train.

The fates seemed to agree.

A door opened and someone grabbed her outstretched hand. The strength of a navvy hauled her aboard to fall panting on the opposite seat. On the end of the strong arm was a doll with a bell of dark hair and a poppy-painted mouth. Apart from the doll, the compartment was empty. Ruth saw now that it was a corridor train, one of the old type, with separate carriages.

As she slumped there, gasping, the idiotic thought occurred to her that tilted from the vertical her rescuer looked as if she would say in a high-pitched monotone, 'Mama.'

Hell's bells, Sister Silke! You're hallucinating with fatigue!

Ruth pressed a hand to her chest and, being a fit and healthy young woman of twenty-six, soon had her rasping breaths under control. When she could speak she managed a jocular, 'You've saved my life!'

'All part of the service,' smiled the doll, revealing little pearly teeth. For all her porcelain appearance she had a cheerfully normal sort of voice. 'Anyway, I saw you flying along, and I hate travelling alone in these old trains. I think most women do.'

And most women haven't got that kind of muscle. Not unless they're nurses . . . Ruth's smile of agreement stretched into a yawn and her hand came up politely to conceal it. Her sleeve reeked of cigarette smoke. Great! All she needed. Sighing, she got back on her sore feet, shrugged off her best navy Jaeger jacket and gave it a thorough shake.

The dark girl hitched her sleek short skirt and crossed black silken knees, running a critical eye over Ruth's grey pleats and ivory Edwardian-style blouse. Ruth could guess the verdict: boring as chalk. Perfectly suitable for meeting a headmaster and his board of governors. And the school doctor, of course.

The girl now turned her attention back to her copy of the March *Vogue*, frail wrists protruding from the sleeves of her snappy Prince of Wales check suit. A perfect white parting bisected her glossy raven head.

The train was swaying as it picked up speed, travelling eastward through a February landscape of sodden fields and hedgerows with overflowing dykes.

Ruth got out a comb and a mirror and attempted to

smooth down her wretched hair. It was so soft, so fine, so unruly; never at its best after ten hours of being pinned up under a frilly white cap. And she hadn't had time for even a smidge of make-up after changing out of her royal blue uniform and making the dash from Edgbaston to New Street Station. How she *longed* to slip off her sensible navy loafers and put up her weary stockinged feet . . .

She delved again into her capacious handbag. It was brown leather and didn't match her shoes. Too bad. If they wanted a fashion-plate rather than an experienced professional woman then that was their problem. Really, this would be the oddest interview of her nursing career . . . and she wasn't even sure about this school job, though the picture on the Ditchingham House prospectus was a sight more appealing than the bleak scene beyond the train's muddy windows.

'SISTER IN CHARGE OF MEDICAL CENTRE.'

Mum had snipped the ad from her staff-room copy of the *Times Educational Supplement*. Here it was, along with the prospectus and the headmaster's letter. 'Responsible for supervising matters relating to the health and medical treatment of the 200 boarders of Ditchingham House Preparatory School, independent and co-educational. Dr Daniel Gather,'—a nice caring name, that—'our visiting physician, holds regular surgeries. The flat provided for the sister in charge is an inherent part of the medical centre and includes a kitchen, although meals are provided by the catering department.' I'm a good cook, thank you all the same. 'Salary to be adjusted according to the qualifications and experience of the person appointed. *Non-smoker preferred*.' Fair enough, agreed Ruth.

The headmaster's letter had made it perfectly clear that during term-time the school would claim every waking moment of the san sister's day. And that could be no bad thing! Of course, if she got the job the Birmingham house would have to be sold. North Devon would be within an hour's easy drive—which would please Mum, who taught music part-time, was no geographer and considered Brum to be located somewhere in the frozen north.

Her companion was still flicking through *Vogue*. Thankful she wasn't obliged to chat, Ruth closed her eyes, her hands clasped loosely in her lap, the palms smooth and dry, the pulse in her wrist a calm measured throb. She was not at all nervous. No butterflies in the stomach, not even one tiny moth. True, she was by nature calm and self-controlled, but this state of numb indifference was beyond that. It had gone on for almost a year. It was as though Jeff's . . . disappearance . . . had bled her dry of emotion. If she got the job, all well and good. If she didn't, no problem! She'd just stay put and learn to come to terms with being alone again.

'I say!' An animated voice interrupted her reverie.

Ruth opened her eyes. The dark girl was leaning forward, *Vogue* abandoned on the seat beside her, pointing now to the papers in Ruth's lap.

'Isn't that the Ditchingham House prospectus?' she asked. 'Are you a parent?'

For a moment Ruth sat there, stunned into silence. A parent—how ironic! She pulled herself together, shaking her head.

'I'm not——' For an uncharacteristic moment, she

stuttered over her words. 'I've applied for a post at the school.'

'Get away!' In spite of her elegance the dark girl had a robust turn of phrase. '*Not* sister in charge of Sick Bay?'

Feeble nod of affirmation from the weary Ruth Silke.

Pearly white teeth flashed in delight. 'Would you believe,' the girl exclaimed, 'I'm up for that too?'

You'd better believe it, smirked a small voice inside Ruth's cotton-wool head. And programmed for success too, by the looks of her. Still, you weren't particularly keen, were you . . . so you won't be *too* upset?

'I don't check the ads in the ordinary way,' Mum had written, 'so this has got to be fate!' As she remembered this, Ruth's expression was rueful. Sorry to disappoint you, Mother dear, but the omens don't look too promising . . .

She stretched out a hand in greeting to her glamorous rival. 'Ruth Silke,' she introduced herself. 'Night sister at the Shotover Clinic in Edgbaston.' Then the laughter spilled out, so infectious that the dark girl joined in too. 'I must own up!' explained Ruth. 'I took you for someone in the fashion world.'

'Get away!'

Ruth nodded her head vigorously. 'And that accounts for the muscles up your sleeves! The way you whipped me aboard . . . But I can't seem to picture you in uniform. Navy blue?'

'Navy blue.' The hand grasping hers was just as thoroughly scrubbed as her own, the nails just as sensibly short and unvarnished. A nurse's hand—unmistakable.

Suzie Lake introduced herself, sharp black eyes noting, but not commenting on, the wedding-ring on Ruth's long, slim fingers. 'I'm a junior casualty sister at the infirmary,' she volunteered. 'And this is the sort of accident I can do with, our bumping into each other like this. We'll share a taxi out to Ditchingham House.'

Now the ice was broken, Suzie was turning into a compulsive talker who required little in the way of feedback. All Ruth had to do was sit quiet and look interested, which wasn't difficult in such vivacious company.

The life story of Suzie Lake seemed wholly charmed: voted by the university the prettiest student nurse in Bristol, pictured as an eighteen-year-old flashing black stockings as she draped herself over a ventilator for an ad in a medical journal. It sounded as if Suzie had everything going for her right where she was, one of the youngest sisters in a teaching hospital. Fancy her wanting to leave!

Ruth ventured to say so. Seeing the tired blue eyes were genuinely puzzled, Suzie became serious. 'Cas is no picnic these days and my father—he's retired from general practice now, well, I'm the youngest of four and we're pretty spread out—he thinks I should go back to nursing children. I've got this gigantic bruise on my upper arm where some drunk grabbed hold of me last Saturday night. I tell you, in my job you need muscles and danger money!'

Ruth looked so concerned and alarmed that Suzie had the grace to blush. 'Well, look,' she confided, 'that's not the whole story. There's this guy ... one of the registrars, and he's married—oh, and it's one of those messes, you know the sort of thing, I really must make the break and get away.' Suzie sighed heavily over the romantic chaos of her affairs, fingers locked about an elegant knee, scanning Ruth's face for a glimmer of disapproval but finding none.

Emboldened, she said, 'But tell me, Ruth, what about you? Are you escaping from something too . . .? No, I guess not, you look so calm and in control of your life.' Again she observed the wedding-ring, those unremarkable clothes concealing curves which the women's mags were currently declaring back in fashion. Though she'll never find out if she only reads the *Nursing Times*! criticised Suzie from her sophisticated vantage-point. Now if I were her I'd go for a bouncy short cut to show off that natural wave . . . she's fair and it's the real thing, and her skin's fabulous. She's OK without much make-up, but she could use a bit of concealer to mask the shadows under her eyes . . . and there's something else there. Something wrong. I think she's sad about something, deep down, for all she's so calm and capable-looking.

'What about you?' she probed again as Ruth hesitated. 'You must get lots of famous people at your clinic.'

Ruth agreed vaguely that from time to time there were some VIP patients. But generally, she shrugged . . .

'A sight more interesting,' Suzie interrupted fervently, 'than grazed knees and bruised heads.' She smiled her delicious smile, crossed black-silk knees and leaned back to enjoy the rest of the journey. Confidence bounced off her in sharp rays, puncturing the thin balloon of optimism which had cushioned Ruth from fatigue. She yawned and tiredly rubbed her forehead.

The perceptive Suzie reacted with professional concern. 'Don't tell me you were on duty last night! I say, that's a bit off.'

Ruth managed a ghost of a smile. 'You know how it is—short-staffed. I'll be fine once we get there. The adrenalin will start to flow and they'll never guess I haven't been to bed since Tuesday night.'

'I'd better shut up and let you have a snooze. Go on—don't worry, I'll wake you when we're nearly there.'

What a kind person, thought Ruth with warm appreciation. All the same, it would never do. 'If I go out for the count I shall feel awful when I wake. Keep talking, Suzie, that's the best thing. Where did you get that absolutely stunning suit?'

Suzie wiggled her padded shoulders and beamed. 'It's a Paul Costello, borrowed from my sister. Makes me feel very *confident* and powerful. I say, I'm dying for a smoke—you don't mind, do you? It helps calm my nerves.'

A cigarette was produced and lighted before you could say Jack Robinson. On the window a big red notice ordered 'No Smoking'. 'Now did I tell you that Mike was at medical school with Dan Gather . . . you know, the school doctor?' Waving aside spirals of smoke, Suzie went on, 'They haven't kept in touch, though. Mike's in hospital medicine and very tied up in London. He said I should mention his name . . .'

Leaning forward confidentially, she went on, 'Dr Gather is said to be *highly dishy*! Two women medical students actually had a fight over him. Can you imagine? Real hair-pulling stuff, according to Mike. Daniel picked them up and dumped them in the physiotherapy swimming-pool to cool off. He eventually married some French girl he met in Lyons.

'But it's very sad. Apparently his wife died tragically young. Mike didn't know the circumstances. So-o . . .' Suzie raised a significant eyebrow, 'there's an opportunity for a nice girl.'

'Nice girl, beware!' muttered Ruth *sotto voce*. Dr Gather sounds like a rolling stone, gathering where he may. Just the kind I couldn't work with. Oh well, the old boys' network will ensure that Sister Lake gets the job. It's all sewn up.

What a waste of time and energy! Indignation fired a small slow burn and Ruth could feel its throbbing begin in her temples. Her lips tightened and her fingers reached up to probe the ache. To have come all this way . . . In itself the emotion was real enough to startle her—*now*, of all times, to discover the prickings of anger! It was like pinching a statue and discovering flesh and blood under a marble skin.

For the past year she had displayed a mask of determined optimism that Jeff would come back to her, damming her feelings, numb with disbelief, working on with the efficiency of a robot . . .

Ruth sighed heavily. For Suzie's sake she might as well go on with it, endure the charade of being interviewed so that Suzie Lake could honourably make the break and escape from that married man who was messing up her life. Besides, there was the prospect of a decent lunch . . .

* * *

The taxi drove through the tiny village of Ditchingham and bowled along an avenue of leafless poplars that reminded Ruth of France. The entrance to Ditchingham House was marked by a school signboard and two rather grand stone pillars guarding an open gateway. Ramps slowed the taxi to a crawl as it made its way along a winding driveway. Dense shrubs crowded the left-hand side. On the right, graceful birch trees rising out of a jewelled carpet of gold and purple crocus allowed a glimpse of the playing-fields beyond.

Suzie chatted away. Ruth stared wordlessly about her. After city living her senses felt stunned. The open skies, the unpolluted air, the smell of damp earth. The death of winter and the birth of spring. Her eyes filled with foolish tears and she blinked them away before the other nurse should notice.

'Rugby in winter and cricket in summer,' said Suzie, pointing out the tall posts on the deserted playing fields which lay between the horizontal stretch of school buildings and the country lane. 'Games are very important in boarding schools, gets the little dears nice and tired for bedtime. That must be the main building—see, Ruth? That gorgeous old house—there in the centre with the statue over the doorway.'

'Mmm?' Ruth was mesmerised by those bright drifts of crocus. She winced as seemingly out of nowhere a pair of sturdy legs in fall-down grey socks and hefty black shoes came crashing through the delicate blooms. 'Careful!' she warned, for the child didn't seem aware of flowers or taxi. 'Hey!' she cried again, sharply rapping on the glass with white knuckles.

Too late! The boy pounded on and into their path.

With a curse the driver stamped on his brakes. There was a sickening thud as child and machine made contact and Ruth saw the small body flung on to the shrubbery verge.

Suzie just shrieked, and the heavily built driver began to struggle out from behind the wheel. But Ruth was out of the taxi in a matter of seconds. 'Hold still!' she panted, grasping a wadge of dark blue blazer. 'Let me check if you're——'

The boy struggled with healthy vigour. 'Let me go, you old witch!' he protested in a hoarse and decidedly ungrateful voice. And wrenching himself free, the child crashed on into the shrubbery.

Ruth had never been called *that* before! 'You little monkey!' she gasped. Hesitating for a fraction of a second, she glanced back at Suzie and the driver, shrugged, then followed in hot pursuit.

The taxi meanwhile began to crawl slowly on up the drive, since clearly it could not follow nurse and quarry through the holly and the ivy. The boy knew where he was making for, dodging smartly round prickly mahonias and skirting dripping laurels that whipped Ruth in the face and snatched at her legs. He burst out into the open before a low modern building marked 'Medical Centre', its small parking area occupied by an elderly Ford Fiesta and a spanking new silver BMW. At the sight of the latter the schoolboy gave a whoop of joy and Ruth, running faster than she had in years, almost careered into the back of him, her cheeks stinging and her heartbeats thumping.

'Now just you listen to me, young man!' she exclaimed, grabbing hold of his shoulders and this time determined to hang on. 'You could have been badly injured, and it would have been entirely your own fault. Stand still when I'm talking to you!'

'Let me go! Let go of me!' wailed a face red with outrage and streaked with dirty tears, 'I want to see my dad. Let me go! Dad!' he bellowed, 'Help, Dad! Ow!'

'Oh, for goodness' sake,' muttered Ruth, 'there's not much wrong with someone who can bellow like a little Turk. Hold still while I wipe your face. No, I'm not letting go till I've had a good look at you.'

He had a mop of dark curls and huge dark eyes framed by stubby wet lashes, a tall sturdy child of about nine years old. Grey cord shorts came almost down to his knees, and his mud-stained wool blazer looked new and several sizes too big. The thick material had helped to save his skin. There didn't seem to be a mark on him!

'Tch, I don't know,' said Ruth in mingled relief and exasperation. 'Where's your handkerchief, then?' She leaned down and patted pockets stuffed with marbles, and at that moment an authoritative voice demanded from the doorway, 'What the hell is all this row out here?' And with an ominous calm, 'What d'you think you're doing with my son?'

'Dad!' blubbered the small boy, and with a twist he was free and rushing towards a tall dark silhouette, cannoning into outstretched arms and burying his grubby face against the lowest button of a crisp striped shirt-front, which was as high as his head could reach.

The man placed a protective hand over the curly head and if looks could chill Ruth would have frozen on the spot. She just stared at the pair of them, her shoulders heaving, quite out of breath. 'I am mightily tempted,' she gasped crossly, 'to give your son a thump round the ear'ole!'

'You'd hit a child,' said the tall man contemptuously, 'about the head?'

'About the head!' he repeated, to emphasise the grossness of her supposed threat. Ruth's hackles rose. She'd spoken in the heat of the moment. What sort of monster did he take her for?

But words of explanation refused to come. Her head whirled and she swayed on her feet. 'You—you shouldn't——'

The grim-faced parent was staring at her now, across the few yards that separated them, his eyes as dark as his son's and fixed upon her with naked anger. Ruth swayed again, and her hand went up to her befuddled head.

The man squeezed the boy's shoulders and said something in low tones. 'Brilliant!' said the boy, and skipped over to investigate the silver BMW. His father shoved his hands in his trouser pockets and walked with leisurely purpose over to Ruth, who was in danger of collapsing into the prickly arms of a holly. Preferable, she considered, to a close encounter with the hostile stranger now looking down on her from beneath narrowed eyelids.

He was taller than herself by a good eight inches; around the six-three mark. By keeping her head level with the knot of his tie—red silk with white spots—she was able to avoid direct eye contact. His shirt was grey with white stripes and his suit well tailored in a fine dark fabric. Momentarily forgetting caution, Ruth glanced up and met the regard of narrowed jet-black eyes set beneath a strong-browed, frowning forehead. He had lovely hair, she noticed dizzily . . . thick and wavy, soft-looking, sprinkled with silver . . . Her gaze dropped to an angry mouth with jutting lower lip, too near her own to be studied with equanimity.

In different circumstances it would have registered on the instant that this was a powerfully attractive man. Ruth, though, saw none of it. He must be as much of a twit as his boy. Probably never heard of the Green Cross Code.

'Should take more water with it!' he muttered cynically as she swayed again, grasped her upper arm, bent towards her like a lover—to smell her breath. Ruth's head fell back, her pupils dilating. 'Have you been drinking? If you're on the staff here, young woman, then I shall have words with the headmaster about this little episode.'

This final insult restored Ruth's self-control. 'Have words with whomsoever you please!' she retorted. She pressed her hand against her upper chest, for her heart was beating fit to burst with the chase and now this extraordinary misunderstanding. 'But I would recommend you speak severely to your son about road sense. He took not the slightest bit of notice where he was going—cannoned into my taxi and in my opinion is lucky to be alive. I was simply trying to examine that boy and reassure myself that he's as OK as he appears. If I were you, I should get a doctor to check him for internal injury.'

The boy began to wail.

'OK, Danny!' called his father. 'You're in dead trouble, sunshine. Into the treatment-room and jacket and shorts off. I'll be with you in two ticks.' He propelled the child ahead of them into the building. 'If you'll come with me, Miss . . .?'

'Silke,' said Ruth tiredly, 'Ruth Silke.' For the first time she noticed the sign on the building: 'Medical Centre'. Comprehension began to dawn in her befuddled brain.

Those eyes again, measuring her up and down, missing nothing: the ruin of her best pearl-grey stockings, the scratch on her pale cheek, her mussed-up hair and the purple smudges of fatigue. 'Hell's teeth, but of course! We're all expecting you.'

Ruth felt her hand enveloped in a surprisingly warm and encouraging handshake. An arm rested on her shoulder, steering her across the clinic threshold. 'I'm Daniel Gather. And you, Sister Silke, look like the Wreck of the *Hesperus*.'

CHAPTER TWO

HEAD held high, clinging to the tatters of her dignity, Ruth crossed the threshold of the medical centre. She suspected there was a smudge of mud on the left side of her nose. Dr Gather seemed to be having difficulty in keeping a straight face. 'Well,' he said, rubbing his jaw, then stating the obvious. 'You can't possibly meet the Head looking like that. We're going to have to clean you up somehow.'

He made it sound like one of the seven labours of Hercules. Ruth particularly objected to the *we*. And it wasn't much fun being stared at with blatant curiosity by an extremely well-dressed and contemptuous man. Gritting her teeth, she ripped a leafless twig from the tangles of her hair. She couldn't look *that* bad, for heaven's sake!

'Wait here,' he said with an inexcusable chuckle. 'I'll root out Matron and see if you can use her quarters to . . . um . . .'

Here followed a graphic pause that turned Ruth's cheeks a ripe shade of Humiliation Pink.

'. . . sort yourself out a bit,' finished Dr Gather.

Ruth peered about for a mirror so that she could inspect the damage for herself, but nothing met her eyes other than blank cream-painted walls and an expanse of polished black-and-white vinyl floor tiles. No gilt-framed water-colours; no comfortable chairs; no elegant tables with tasteful floral arrangements. Very different from a private nursing home, this school medical centre.

The doctor disappeared to the left of the passageway that faced her, and was gone for several minutes.

Ruth waited restlessly.

A loud snivel caught her attention and she realised it came from behind the door of the treatment-room where young Master Gather was awaiting his father's attention. Again the snivel, and Ruth guessed with a sympathetic smile that the child had lost his handkerchief. Fearing for the sleeve of his blazer, she stepped quietly over and pushed the door ajar. Danny had hitched himself up on to the high treatment couch and was happily swinging his legs over the edge, apparently, in spite of his runny nose, in no great fear of his father's wrath. And doubtless, thought Ruth drily, enjoying missing his lessons! 'Wagging it', they had called it in her own schooldays at the comprehensive . . . remember that terrifying maths teacher they'd called The Fist? But she'd never played truant, however great the temptation. The 'flight or fight' syndrome it was: student nurses learned about it as part of their eight weeks' psychiatric training. She wondered what class Danny Gather was supposed to be in now.

Danny stiffened in apprehension. His eyes, dark as his father's, looked huge within a small face smeared by grimy hands. The snivels were the remnants of a cold.

'Blow!' ordered Ruth, supplying a large tissue from an opened packed left on top of a locked cabinet. 'What have you been studying this morning . . . coal mining?'

The child snorted a giggle and scraped ineffectively

at his face.

'For goodness' sake!' sighed Ruth.

Danny watched suspiciously as she went over to the sink, ran the tap and then advanced on him brandishing a damp wadge of soft paper. Grasping his curly head with a firm hand, she made a thorough job of it, standing back to approve the shining pink skin which now emerged. 'And now I suppose you think *I* look worse than you do, young man!' she chided in mock-scolding tones.

'Matron's going to have an eppy when she sees the floor!' The boy cupped a delighted hand over his chuckles. 'And you've done it as much as me!' he squirmed. 'Oh, brilliant!'

Oh, hell! cursed Ruth to herself. The trail of muddy footsteps zigzagged over the spick and span treatment-room, squidged across the hall and out to the clinic entrance. Ruth hopped on one foot, inspecting the soles of shoes coated with mud from that dash through the bushes.

'Have you come for Matron's job?' asked the boy with new interest. 'I hope you get it. You're much prettier than Matron.'

'Shan't get it now, shall I?' said Ruth with a wry smile, stepping out of her loafers. 'Better hop back on my broomstick and——'

She broke off, hearing voices approaching, padding back into the entrance hall on stockinged feet just as Dr Gather and Matron rounded the corner. Matron's face was a study in distaste. The floor and Ruth's laddered legs drew her eyes downward on a hiss of horrified dragon-breath.

Daniel Gather introduced the two nurses with a smooth amusement that had Ruth gritting her small white teeth.

'*Mrs* Silke,' she corrected him firmly, '*Ruth* Silke.'

The doctor quirked an eyebrow and seemed about to say something . . . then changed his mind and, going into the treatment-room, closed the door behind him, leaving Ruth to face alone this tartar of the old Nightingale régime.

Miss McCarthy, who from the first had been known as 'Matron', was retiring, extremely unwillingly, after twenty-six years at Ditchingham House. 'Once a nurse, always a nurse' was her motto. And if it had not been for her reaching the Royal College of Nursing's compulsory retirement age, her robust constitution would have seen Miss McCarthy running the 'School Sanitorium' until the century she confidently expected to reach. She had seen headmasters come and go, and the building of the new medical centre had been carried out under her eagle eye. In fact that eagle eye and the severe navy dress and large white muslin cap with its two floating wings reminded Ruth of illustrations of battleaxe matrons of illustrious London hospitals . . . back in the days when girls had to *pay* for the privilege of SRN training!

'You'd better come with me,' said Matron heavily. 'You can use my bathroom. As Dr Gather says, you can't possibly be interviewed looking like that.' Not that it will make much difference, her manner implied.

Dangling her muddy shoes and following meekly in that starchy wake, Ruth couldn't help but feel sympathy for Miss McCarthy. Ditchingham House had been her home for all these years. It must be very sad to be obliged to step down and make way for a younger and —let's face it, bound to be!—far less experienced nurse.

The passage to the right turned out to lead to the resident nurse's living quarters. 'Go through my bedroom. You will find a clean towel and everything you need.'

'Thank you,' said Ruth gratefully, astonished by the spartanly furnished bedroom, which was more like a nun's cell. The white paintwork, however, was fresh and the beige carpet immaculately Hoovered, the ensuite bathroom not exactly cheerless, but totally lacking any feminine touches. Ruth knew there was a kitchen and sitting-room besides, but no suggestion was made that she should be shown these rooms, so she suspected wryly that Matron had relegated her to the bottom of the list and was not going to waste any more time than was necessary on the disreputable Ruth Silke. There must be a ward for sick pupils at the other end of the passage, and though Ruth itched to have a proper look at everything, she knew that she must quickly rescue her appearance and get along to the headmaster's drawing-room.

The other candidates were all drinking sherry before a buffet lunch and a formal tour of the school and medical centre, to be followed by the interviews. Of the five on the short list, one had withdrawn, leaving Suzie Lake, Ruth herself, a middle-aged motherly woman with grey hair who seemed to Ruth the ideal candidate and who was conversing fluently with Matron whose winged cap was bouncing in agreement; and finally a thin dark woman who looked very nervous and whose sherry glass was visibly shaking as she stood with the headmaster.

Ruth found herself in a large and rather grand room where at least a dozen people were gathered in amiable conversation. It was all very civilised. A log fire burned in the cavern of the fireplace and the room was well lit by two huge windows which must be murder to curtain, they reached so high. Antiques and oil-paintings and urns of dried flowers met her gaze, and, glancing round for him, Ruth spied Daniel Gather with Suzie Lake, Suzie smiling up at the tall doctor over the rim of her sherry glass, laying an uninhibited hand on his sleeve and clearly to be heard saying, 'How perfectly amazing! Isn't it a small world? You must come over, Dan. Mike says you and he were particularly . . .'

'Mrs Silke—how do you do?'

Ruth turned to find at her elbow a small slight woman in a tweed skirt and silk blouse with a cameo brooch at the neck, extending her right hand in greeting.

'Dan warned us you'd be delayed. I'm Gwyneth Raven, the headmaster's wife. It's rather warm in here, so why don't you slip out of your jacket? Help yourself to a glass of sherry and come and meet my husband.'

Leaving her jacket on a chair, and against her better judgement but out of politeness, Ruth accepted a small dry sherry. She never drank very much; and in the daytime it only made her tired and flushed her fair skin. Like the dormouse at the Mad Hatter's tea-party in *Alice in Wonderland*, she might fall asleep with her head on the table. The final calamity to crown a calamitous day. But what the hell? Since she was out of the running she might as well enjoy herself. Ruth took a sip and her palate responded with pleasure. She took another and felt even better, raising her glass in a small mocking gesture at Dr Gather, who had his back to the window and was looking directly at her now, examining her with an intent black gaze before the glamorous Suzie Lake reclaimed his interest.

He winked. Ruth was so taken aback she almost spilled her lovely drink.

Gwyneth Raven had a Welsh accent so lilting that Ruth listened to the sound of her voice without really taking in the potted history she was being given of Ditchingham House. The headmaster joined them and heartily pumped Ruth's hand. She'd been expecting an older man, but Charles Raven was possibly much the same age as Daniel Gather, shorter and more stockily built, with thinning light brown hair and an affable and welcoming manner. The Ravens, decided Ruth, accepting a refill of this quaffable sherry, were a charming couple, and more than made up for the frosty attitude of the matron and the doctor.

'Yes, I met Dr Gather earlier,' she acknowledged, deliberately non-committal. And not wishing to get the doctor's son in hot water for being out of lessons, she explained that her taxi had dropped her first at the medical centre and that Daniel Gather had been there at the time.

'Such a kind and caring man,' enthused Gwyneth with real sincerity.

Ruth raised her eyebrows in a gesture that could be taken for anything but which in fact was registering that she found this pretty hard to swallow.

'We couldn't be more fortunate in our medical officer, could we, darling? He sends his children here, you know. Little Danny—he's seven now, nearly eight, and he's in Mrs Sugden's class. And four-year-old Rosie started this term in our pre-prep department. It makes a break for Beatrice——'

'Oh, excuse me, they want us to go in for the buffet. Charles! Can you make the announcement? . . .'

Several of the school governors had joined them and one held Ruth back for several moments, questioning her about her past experience, so that she was one of the last to leave the drawing-room with its chintz armchairs, crackling log fire and tall windows looking out over the playing-fields. So Dr Gather had married again, she mused. How disappointing for Suzie! And as for 'little' Danny—what were they feeding seven-year-olds these days? Raw steaks? The child was obviously going to grow up as big and handsome as his father, but with luck, under the tutelage of Ditchingham House, with a good deal more charm than his doctor dad.

The lunch was filling if unexciting; just what Ruth needed to blot up two glasses of sherry and stop her stomach rumbling. And she found herself genuinely interested and full of questions during the tour of the school, led by the headmaster and the bursar, a military-looking man in his fifties who explained that he was responsible for the financial side of things, including payment of salaries. The tour was very comprehensive and included the main admin building and the boarding houses and teaching areas as well as the rather grandly titled medical centre—which everyone except Charles Raven seemed to refer to as

Sick Bay.

The candidates were told that Matron had several part-time staff assisting, to cover both day and night duty, and it was possible that a pre-nursing student would join the school for the summer term. Ruth had not been aware that there would be other trained nurses working under the direction of the sister in charge, and this added a further dimension of interest to the post, for she enjoyed teamwork and the responsibility of staff management.

'And of course,' Matron reminded the four of them, singling out Ruth for a heavily significant glare, 'as the advertisement made *quite* clear, a non-smoker will be preferred.' In puzzlement Ruth turned round to see if there was someone standing behind her. Suzie said nothing but caught Ruth's eye and pulled a face: no one was going to tell *her* what she might or might not do!

The order of interviews was announced, and Ruth, being an S and near the end of the alphabet, found herself last in the line.

To pass the time she decided a brisk walk would do her the world of good; the crisp country air would clarify her thoughts and keep tiredness at bay, and she'd see something of the children, whose shrill voices could be heard out on the playing-fields.

A weak sun was breaking fitfully through low cloud and there were girls in Aertex blouses and navy shorts on the netball courts and boys in red-and-white striped shirts on the rugger pitches. Sometimes a lone child came along on an errand for a teacher, bestowing on Ruth a beaming smile and a 'hello!' to which she responded gladly and which cheered her no end. There was a big swimming-pool, she saw, but it was covered over for the winter months with a plastic dome. And the netball courts were marked out for tennis in the summer. In a few months the extensive grounds would be a sight for sore eyes: and Ruth had certainly got a couple of those after the smoky journey from Birmingham!

Her interview was timed for two forty-five, so at two-thirty she made her way to the cloakroom already pointed out to her, next door to the committee-room where the assembled governors were waiting with the headmaster and the medical officer and the matron. Inspecting her laddered stockings, Ruth decided there was only one thing for it—to take them off and be interviewed bare-legged! Standing up, her skirt hid the worst; sitting down was a different matter. And she couldn't possibly explain to the interviewing panel how she came to be in such a pickle.

It was only when the flushing of the lavatory died away to silence that Ruth, washing her hands and critically examining her reflection in the mirror, to her consternation realised there were voices speaking on the other side of the wall. And that she could hear every word being said . . .

'I don't care what she's put on her application forms——,' Matron was holding forth '—the girl reeks of cigarette smoke! And you know as well as I do that it really will not do in a school sanatorium . . . *medical* centre, then, Charles, whatever you want to call it. In my day it was the san, and for the life of me I don't know why you needed to mess around altering things.'

Keeping a tight rein on his patience, which Miss McCarthy tended to put very much to the test, the headmaster repeated for the umpteenth time that parents found it reassuring to know the school had a fully equipped medical centre and a medical officer on call, and that all the nursing staff were registered general nurses. As for the smoking business, they could hardly accuse Ruth Silke of being a liar.

Within the cloakroom, Ruth's mouth fell open and her heart began to thud against her ivory blouse. She'd naturally assumed it was Suzie who was being discussed, for at twenty-six and after all she'd been through Ruth no longer considered herself a 'girl'. And she'd never smoked in her life! She sniffed the sleeve of her jacket, but—thank heaven for that!—the brisk walk had blown the stale whiff of the businessmen's smoke right away. Matron had been jumping to conclusions. She really was an unjust woman!

Ruth began to feel hopping angry. She'd have dearly liked to rap on the wall and shout. 'How dare you?' But of course it was hardly the done thing to eavesdrop . . .

This is so humiliating! she raged, her usually mild temperament thrown right out of gear. I'm going to hear the rest of this. And then I'm going in there to tell them just what to do with their wretched job!

Dr Gather spoke next, and it was clear from his tone that he considered his precious time was being wasted. 'Then we ask her outright if she smokes or not and the hell with it. If she says yes, then we offer the job to the London candidate in spite of her hay fever. Right? Miss Lake is not sufficiently experienced in staff management: and besides, I feel that this would not be a wise career move for a girl of her potential. That other woman hasn't the authority for the job. Handling kids

is no soft option, as she ought to have realised. Which
leaves us with Mrs Silke, who for me, on paper, is the
pick of the bunch.'

Ruth gasped in astonishment, her anger going right
off the boil. The pick of the bunch, he'd said!

The doctor's deep voice continued. 'Where's her
husband, by the way? Anyone know?'

Ruth bit her lip and dug her nails into her palms. A
sudden rush of tears flooded her eyes and quivered on
the long lashes. In that instant she felt very, very lonely.
Where *was* her husband? Whatever had possessed her
to think she could do this? What if one day Jeff should
come home, only to find she had sold up and gone
away? How would he find her . . .? She couldn't! After
all, she couldn't. And it sounded as if she was going to
be offered this wretched job, with Daniel Gather, senior
and junior, and that spartan set of living quarters, and
all these . . . well-meaning, no doubt, but still strangers,
when all was said and done. And really it was Suzie who
wanted, who needed to get away, who would be so
disappointed if . . .

Get a grip of yourself, Ruth Silke! ordered her
rational *alter ego*. Face the facts. You know Jeff's never
coming back. You agreed when Mum advised a
complete change of scenario. Who's to say your need
isn't as great as Suzie Lake's? She'll pick up another
post without difficulty. So would you, if it comes to that,
but in spite of everything you like the feel of this place
and you know that you could be happy here . . . once
you get the measure of Daniel Gather. What's it going
to be, then? Flight or fight?

Ruth gripped the edge of the washbasin and, looking

into her own reflected eyes, willed herself back into calm control.

Her hands were steady as she took out her make-up bag and applied Rose Clarinette lipstick, blotting with a tissue until a natural veil of colour remained, her mouth soft and full. For someone who had been so long without sleep, her eyes, a soft violety blue, were remarkably lustrous—it must have been that momentary flood of tears. The damp air had tamed her fluffy hair and the bruise-coloured shadows under her eyes gave her face a worldly and authoritative air. Capable she looked, and capable she was. And if Ditchingham House wants me, decided Ruth with a resolute tilt of her chin, I'll put the past behind me and gladly work my butt off for these children.

'Are you divorced, Mrs Silke?' asked the chairman of governors—who was also the Vicar of Ditchingham—after the post had been offered and accepted.

'I'm a widow,' said Ruth without a qualm.

'I'm so sorry,' said the chairman quietly, and Dan Gather had the grace to lower his cool stare to the doodle he'd been making on the back of an envelope. The chairman stood and reached across the sea of polished mahogany to grasp Ruth warmly by the hand. 'We shall look forward to welcoming you in time for the summer term . . .'

Daniel Gather insisted on driving them back to Bath station in his brand new silver BMW.

Ruth sat quietly in the back, exhilaration mingling

with sheer exhaustion so that it was easier not to speak but just collapse into a comfortable silence. It was incredible that she could have built up such a hard, impervious shell of self-protection. In her heart of hearts she must have been wanting this job very badly—but hadn't allowed herself to acknowledge her own need. Now her luck was changing and there would be good days ... months ... years even!... ahead. Her chest felt tight with emotion at the prospect of a kind of happiness again.

'Super car!' said Suzie, tight skirt riding up around her silky black thighs as she settled into luxuriant leather. 'Mmm ... wonderful brand-new smell! Didn't Mike tell me you used to drive a two-seater Morgan?'

Dan took his eyes off the road. 'Ah, those carefree bachelor days. I could tell you a tale or two about your brother.'

'He's already told me a tale or two about *you*,' warned Suzie.

Wow! thought Ruth, her wool-gathering interrupted by the vibes between these two in front.

Daniel Gather intercepted Suzie's provocative sidelong glance with an unabashed quirk of an eyebrow.

Show-off! frowned a nervous Ruth, who had only recently learned to drive. It'll be, 'Look, no hands' next!

But Suzie's vivacious laughter made her join in with a smile. Considering the outcome of the day, the glamour-girl nurse was still in buoyant spirits. Which only goes to show what a nice person Suzie is, Ruth sighed with relief, not sulking or making me feel awkward ...

No wonder Dan Gather is so attracted to her, she

mused wistfully.

Again his face was in profile, turned towards his vivacious passenger. He had just the sort of thick, soft, slightly waving hair Ruth decided she liked most, worn slightly long—probably just because he hadn't had time to get to a barber, or his wife hadn't reminded him—so that it curled on the nape of his head. There was quite a lot of grey in it, especially over the temples, and she could see the darkness of beard beneath his smooth olive skin. A deep line running from nose to mouth gave him a fascinating severity that made her shiver as she remembered his anger that morning, that same face bending over hers and those hands on the steering-wheel gripping her two arms with violence. The memory was so powerful that her right hand flew to the left sleeve of her jacket as if to massage an actual pain.

With a start Ruth realised that his eyes in the driving mirror were looking straight into hers. He tilted his head back slightly, speaking across his shoulder to include her in the conversation.

'Danny saw the new car this morning when his class was walking across to chapel. Couldn't resist temptation, the scamp. He skipped Woodwork to come and approve the goods. Sorry he gave you such a fright.'

Ruth was too tired for circumspection. And she certainly didn't want this future colleague sensing the effect he was *already* having on her pulse-rate! So she responded rather sharply to what might have been intended as an olive branch.

'I hope you gave him a good ticking off. I don't want that sort of carry-on every time you visit the medical centre.'

Two steel-black eyes trapped hers in the driving mirror. Their expression was ominous. Telling me my job as a parent? they challenged. Just try it, Sister Silke!

'You'll be pleased to know,' Dr Gather continued smoothly, 'that Danny came to no harm. Apart from being somewhat—shaken up.'

The last two words were given special emphasis. Ruth bit her lip.

He was ignoring her suggestion that his errant son should get a good ticking off. She didn't want the poor kid punished—just made to take more care in future. But it was difficult to argue with the back of the doctor's neck. Mind your own business, nurse! was the clear implication.

'Phew, that's a relief!' exclaimed Suzie. 'Your little boy gave us an awful fright, you know, Dan. Ruth was absolutely marvellous—out of the taxi and after him while I and the driver were still gibbering with shock! You've got reactions like lightning, Ruth. But didn't he lead you a dance? Really, it's hilarious when you come to think about it.'

Silently Ruth rolled her eyes to heaven. Ha ha ha.

'No damage done,' agreed Dr Gather heartily, displaying an irritating lack of concern for Ruth herself.

'Only to my stockings!' she muttered rebelliously, wishing a moment later that she'd had the sense to hold her tongue.

'Your sto-ckings . . .' drawled Dan Gather, raising an amused eyebrow. 'You wear stockings? Then you're a woman after my own heart, Sister Silke. Are you a woman after my own heart too, Miss Lake?'

'Oh, definitely, Dr Gather,' purred Suzie. 'I think most of us find tights too hot on the wards nowadays. I know I do. But stockings with a skirt *this* short—well, you do see my problem . . .'

'He's a dish.'

'He's outrageous!'

'Ruth,' giggled Suzie, 'he was pulling your leg. Where's your sense of humour?'

'Under my pillow!' yawned Ruth. She was silent for a moment, then murmured her thoughts aloud, her head lolling back against the seat, her troubled eyes on the darkening countryside beyond the train's mud-slicked windows. 'I wonder if I've been sensible . . .'

If she hadn't heard Dan Gather with her own ears, she'd have assumed he must have been overruled in his choice of his old friend's sister as the new school nurse. But what had been his actual words? Something like, 'Mrs Silke for me . . . the pick of the bunch.' Ruth knew she ought to be more pleased, but in view of their verbal skirmish that morning it was nothing short of confusing.

She tugged her skirt over her bare legs. She would have to be very wary indeed when she started working with him. 'I wonder if I've done the right thing?' she mused aloud. 'There's bound to be conflict. He's the sort who would never consider another's point of view. Oh, I don't know!' she sighed gustily. 'Men doctors can be so *arrogant*!'

'Dead right!' agreed Suzie with cheerful lack of filial loyalty. 'Daddy was an absolute autocrat when we were kids. God help us if we stepped out of line. My mother's a saint, which helps, of course—she's rather like you, as a matter of fact, Ruth, calm and composed and reassuring. No, I'm not at all surprised you got the job,' she rattled on, silencing Ruth's embarrassed protests and in no sense dampened by her own unsuccessful day. 'You're perfect for it. I see now, I just wouldn't have the patience with all those kids. As for the wicked Dr Gather —that Matron believes he's St Luke himself, so he can't be as diabolical as all that. And frankly, my dear, the feller's quite exceptionally attractive. *And*, more to the point, available——'

'But Beatrice——!' Ruth interrupted.

'Blow *Beatrice*!' Airily Suzie waved aside that little objection.

Ruth lapsed back into a doubtful silence.

'Let's face it,' said Suzie, delving into her bag and lighting up another cigarette, 'Dan's a breath of fresh air after all those pallid, overworked hospital medics. A rare hunk, you must admit. I wouldn't kick him out of bed,' she added naughtily, 'would you?'

Ruth gulped. Just how uninterested she was in the sexuality of her medical colleague, Suzie could never know; and now was not the moment for making a clean breast of her most private affairs.

Changing the subject, so tired now that she was almost inarticulate, Ruth struggled to convey her feelings of concern for Suzie's future. After all, this was to have been a fresh start for the casualty sister; and the fact that Suzie was so smitten with Dan Gather only made matters worse . . .

Again her halting words of apology were waved aside. Ruth was puzzled. This was more than politeness: Suzie truly didn't care.

'So they didn't select me—no problem.'

With lowered eyelids and a small private smile, Suzie toyed with a pearl earring . . . then in a breathtaking rush took Ruth into her confidence.

'Listen, you've no need to lose any sleep on my account. Now we're on our own, I can tell you!' The black eyes glittered with pent-up excitement. 'Because after lunch Dan and I took a stroll outside, and you'll never guess what he suggested——'

She hesitated dramatically, and Ruth, who couldn't imagine what was coming next, held her breath . . .

CHAPTER THREE

THERE were two things Ruth was going to have to get used to: sleeping on the ground floor, and sleeping in a single bed.

Making a very early start of it, she had hired a transit van and driven the most precious of her belongings rather gingerly down the motorway, leaving the small house in Bournville in the care of two nursing colleagues. Right at this moment, selling number eleven seemed too painful to contemplate. And what if . . . but no, she warned herself, tight-lipped; as the days and months passed by the whole situation became more and more hopeless.

With the help of Angus Stewart, the junior games master—six feet of hunky muscle and brawn and still tanned from a late skiing trip, as was evident from the white singlet he was sporting with his tracksuit bottoms—the van was emptied of every last book and cooking pot. Ruth eventually succeeded in persuading the very attentive Angus that she really could manage now and that yes, the electric drill was hers—Jeff's, in fact, but she didn't want to go into explanations—and that yes, she could indeed sort out the wiring up of the compact disc player *and* fix the shelves in the sitting-room.

It had been a long day. Dusk was beginning to fall.

Ruth spread newspapers to catch the spill of dust, then drilled carefully into the marks she had pencilled in on the wall. Each small hole she plugged with a Rawlplug, and then came the awkward task of screwing the metal uprights into place. Another pair of hands would have been useful, but managing alone was something you got used to if your husband spent long periods away from home—and anyway, Ruth was a natural for coping. She stepped back and surveyed her handiwork, rubbing at the aching muscles in her arms as she decided where the brackets were to go. A big shelf lower down for cookery books and her sewing basket, nursing textbooks within easy reach and compact discs likewise, paperbacks in alphabetical order on the higher shelves . . .

It was getting chilly in the darkening room, so she switched on one bar of the electric fire and the two wall lights. To the strains of Elgar—the compact discs were mostly Jeff's choice, but anyway Ruth felt like some Elgar here in the heart of the English countryside—she began fixing the bookshelves, and only gradually became aware of a loud and unmusical knocking at the hall door just along the passage. Stopping the music with the remote control gadget, she went to investigate.

With the san itself empty and another week to go before the official start of the summer term, Ruth could have locked the main door and no one would have begrudged her wanting to stem the steady stream of well-wishers who had been popping in and out to say 'Hi!' and 'Welcome!' and 'Anything we can do to help?' As far as Ruth was concerned all these friendly faces were a delight, and she'd no intention of locking up until she went to bed—indeed, she felt far safer here than in Birmingham, surrounded by the burgeoning shrubbery and with nothing but fresh green fields stretching beyond the extent of the Ditchingham House grounds.

Wiping her hands on her dusty jeans, her hair twisted up and held in an untidy mass by a big red plastic clip, she opened the door, her tired features transformed by the beautiful smile which even now Angus Stewart was thinking of as he jogged round the perimeter of the cricket field. He liked nurses and he had this vision of them as unfazed practical women who could turn a hand to anything. And he specially liked blondes. Sister Silke more than fitted the bill. And hadn't his father said at Christmas, 'It's about time you stopped playing around, Angus, and settled down. If you want to be a housemaster you'll have to get married pretty sharpish.'

Two children stood in the doorway, looking rather uncertain of their welcome even though they were carrying the new san sister's supper. 'Have you been knocking long? I am sorry!' apologised Ruth, drawing them into the narrow passage with an arm on each little girl's shoulder. 'It's Jane and Julia, isn't it? Come and see how I'm getting on——'

She led the way to the kitchen and the identical twins, long fair plaits dangling over red sweatshirts, trooped after her carrying between them a basket covered with a linen tea-towel.

'Mrs Raven sent you some supper,' they volunteered in unison, four blue eyes glancing curiously round the cluttered kitchen. In the Dragon's day this was definitely out of bounds. No pupil was ever known to have crossed the Dragon's threshold . . . Julia looked at Jane and both giggled . . . and lived! Ruth smiled too. Yes, wasn't it just chaos?

Ruth had already met these two, the nine-year-old daughters of Mr Wrigglesby, the housemaster of St Philip's. Several families of the teaching staff lived on the premises for most of the year round and for these children Ditchingham House was home. Never a dull moment, just as Ruth had hoped.

In the basket was a plate of roast beef sandwiches, apples, bananas, and a thermos flask of tomato soup. 'Isn't that kind?' exclaimed Ruth. 'I hadn't realised how late it was. And I'm absolutely starving!'

'Mrs Raven said you'd be very busy and we should bring you something to eat——' started Jane, and Julia finished for her,

'——but we're not to bother you and be in the way.'

Ruth opened the fridge and took out a carton of Jaffa juice. 'You're not bothering me at all,' she reassured her young visitors. 'Stay and talk to me—that's if it isn't coming up to your bedtime.'

The little girls settled happily on high stools with frosty glasses of orange juice. 'We don't go to bed till half-past eight in the holidays,' volunteered Julia, the more confident twin. 'And Dr Gather's come to see Mummy, so Dad said go over to the games-room or "Do something constructive, the pair of you!"' Comically she mimicked her father's voice.

The soup was very hot. And Dr Gather was on the premises. Both, in their way, unexpected.

Ruth's first thought was: I hope he's not planning on coming round here with another dose of verbal aggro! All I'm craving for is a soak in a steaming Radox bath with that very up-to-date accident and emergency textbook I ordered from Hudson's.

Her second was to wonder if she could offer the family any further help herself. She blew thoughtfully on her soup. 'Is your mother unwell?' she asked, keeping her tone of voice casual and unalarming.

'Don't think so,' said Julia brightly. 'Dr Gather often pops in at night.'

Jane's voice was a whisper of excitement. 'We're getting a new baby sister on May the ninth!'

Julia gave a dramatic sigh and rolled her blue eyes to the ceiling. 'Silly! A baby doesn't get born on a particular day. It could be overdue or *anything*.' While the girls bickered gently Ruth chewed a speculative lip.

'We know it's going to be a sister,' confided Jane, quieter and shyer than her twin, her eyes wide and her hands gripping the stool's edge, 'because Mummy had the am-amni——'

'Amniocentesis?' prompted Ruth gently.

'Yes, that's it! The test that shows if the baby's all right and tells if it's a boy or a girl. You have to have it done if you're quite old, don't you, Julia?' she appealed to her sister.

Professional antennae were alerting Ruth to the fact that Jane was a sensitive child; and that she was making a brave effort to conceal her anxiety from her more outgoing sister. Just to show she understood, and was not about to make light of Jane's fears, Ruth said comfortingly that Dr Gather would be taking special care of her mother, as he did of all the children in the school.

''Cept for Danny!' said Julia boldly. 'He's not much good at looking after Danny. Danny's always hurting himself, always having accidents. And his mum *died* having a baby.'

'No, she didn't,' argued Jane. 'It wasn't anything to do with the baby. It was afterwards when she wasn't very well.'

Ruth caught her breath at what the twins were saying. Danny accident prone! And his mother . . .?

'Crisps?' she suggested, to put a stop to the bickering.

'Oh, yes, please!' said the two little gossips eagerly, for all the world as if potato crisps were the greatest treat. 'Can we help you with anything, Sister Silke?'

Stifling a weary yawn, Ruth smiled and shook her head. Goodness, how tired she suddenly felt! 'It's kind of you to offer, but I'm going to bed myself quite soon. In the morning I've got to get the van back to Birmingham and pick up my own car. I think I'll lock up after you two——'

Loud knocking on the hall door interrupted her in mid-sentence.

It was Dr Gather himself, looming large in the doorway and casting a gigantic black shadow behind him. He wore a light-coloured Burberry mac and the shoulders were wet with rain.

'There you are, you two!' Abruptly he addressed the twins across Ruth, ignoring her as she backed against the wall, her heartbeats quickening at the sight of him. 'Your father's looking for you,' he warned in a voice that was considerably less than caring and kindly. 'Off you go. And make it snappy, or you'll get soaked.'

This information galvanised Ruth into action. 'It's raining? I think I left a window open in the van. I'd better just go and check.'

She made to follow the girls, but Dr Gather stepped

in uninvited, blocking the entrance so that she couldn't get past, dominating even this tall girl in the tight squeeze of the passageway.

'You did. And I've closed it.'

'That was kind of you,' she acknowledged, uncomfortably perceiving that the doctor was in rather a bad mood, preoccupied, here out of obligation rather than choice.

He had to duck his head to avoid the bare light bulb dangling from the passage ceiling, and as he did so a lock of hair fell across his wet brow. Raindrops sparkled among the threads of silver and ran down his olive skin, like tears.

A child's voice echoed inside Ruth's head. 'His mum *died* having a baby.' Ruth couldn't bear to think about it. She drew a deep breath and the oddest sensation stabbed her in the ribs. Must have pulled a muscle heaving all those boxes around . . .

'I suppose those two chatterboxes told you I was visiting their mother,' he said brusquely.

'How is Mrs Wrigglesby? If there's any way I can be of help I'd be glad to——'

'You'll have enough on your plate,' was the dour response, and it was obvious to Ruth that she was getting her wrist slapped for taking the demands of her new post over-lightly. 'She'd prefer a home birth, but it's out of the question. Val should be fine, so long as she does as I say.'

The set of his mouth suggested a man who expected his orders to be obeyed. The message in his hard eyes was obvious: That goes for you too, Sister Silke!

Ruth was well used to dealing under pressure with all

types of the medical breed—from the grandest of
consultants down to the greenest of housemen. But Dan
promised to be the most potent challenge yet to her
self-control. She raised an eyebrow and her blue eyes
were very cool.

Without waiting for an invitation Dan Gather stepped
forward. Ruth stepped back. Looking down at her
tumble of fair hair and the rising flush on her smooth
cheek, he waited for her to step aside. What was the
alternative? Ruth did so, pulling a childish face at his
uncaring back.

Hands in his pockets, big and bulky in his damp
raincoat, as if he owned the place, Dan walked into the
kitchen and out of it, into the sitting-room and out of it,
into the bathroom and through into her bedroom. He
seemed very much at ease in *her* domain. And he'd got
a damn cheek, thought Ruth crossly as she saw him pick
up the silver-framed photo from her bedside table,
examine it for a moment and then put it down and stroll
out of her bedroom as she leaned against the wall and
watched him, her mouth and eyes rebellious.

'Well,' he said finally, 'you're a fast worker and no
mistake. I'd supposed you might be in need of a hand.
However, you're clearly handy enough for the both of
us.' Big strapping wench that you are, teased his insolent
eyes.

'Angus Stewart is helping me,' Ruth responded
defiantly, perching herself on the arm of a
cream-upholstered easy chair, leaving him to stand.
Adding, and goodness knows why, for she might have
guessed he would take it provocatively, 'He's been an
absolute *angel*!'

Dan quirked an eyebrow as he summed up Ruth's dishevelled appearance. He trailed his dark gaze downward, from the top of her untidy head with its frivolous red hairclip, lingering over the stubborn pout of the generous mouth and the straining buttons of the much-laundered and slightly shrunken gingham shirt, the faded jeans which clung too tightly at thigh and calf, the bare ankles and feet.

'Good for Angus,' he drawled pointedly. 'But if you think he's an angel then you're in for a nice surprise.'

Ruth jerked herself upright. 'What's that supposed to mean?'

'Whatever you like to make of it,' came the lazy reply. 'I should say you can take pretty good care of yourself, Mrs Silke.' Then, as if to change the subject and cool her down, he nodded towards the new shelves, the newspaper spread carefully over the carpet, the electric drill and the little heap of screws. 'You fix those?'

'Of course.' Ruth's voice was curt and her arms were folded. Strolling in, checking her out as if he had the *droit de seigneur* or something! That wasn't quite the right term, but vaguely she knew it implied arrogance and male superiority and would suffice till in the peace and privacy of her bedtime thoughts she could decide how best to describe her medical colleague.

Dr Gather glanced at her sidelong. 'Didn't think that was Angus's forte,' he said insinuatingly, 'putting up shelves.'

Ruth opened her mouth, goaded now beyond all discretion. If Dan Gather believed he'd got a meek and mild yes-woman in Ruth Silke, he was making an almighty mistake!

'Let's get one thing straight!' she blazed . . .

Too late! For a deliberate finger on the remote control brought Elgar's Second Symphony back into full throttle, the volume increasing until Ruth was driven to fling her hands over her ears and cry out in shocked protest.

He was visibly gloating! She could see it in his sardonic black eyes, in the flash of his strong white teeth, in his brief unsympathetic grin. But he did subdue the head-splitting sound, relish in his voice as with soft emphasis he underlined her vulnerability. 'No one can hear you,' he murmured in that rich, deep, hypnotic voice of his. 'You're entirely on your own over here.'

Ruth's chin lifted in defiance, while under her clothes her body shivered. 'That doesn't worry me,' she claimed in her best sister-in-charge voice, drawing herself up to full height.

'Time for my bath,' she announced pointedly. 'I've had a very grubby day.'

Dan checked his watch. 'And Bea will be wondering where I've got to,' he murmured laconically.

Ruth stared at him in exasperation. Really, his lack of consideration for that poor woman was little short of appalling! 'Oh,' she said sarcastically, 'does she wait up for you?'

He gave her an odd look. Ignoring her question as if it was too childish to be acknowledged, 'I shall see you,' he said, 'on Wednesday after my antenatal clinic. We can get down to some official business.'

With a brusque goodnight he was gone, striding out into the wet black night, leaving Ruth with the vexing sensation of sheer blessed relief to be rid of the turbulent doctor. And regret at the poignant space he left behind.

There was a large expanse of mirror above the bath, presumably to reflect light from the narrow frosted window into the otherwise dark little bathroom. Matron had left a yellowing net curtain in situ.

While the water ran, Ruth took off all her clothes and stared at herself for some moments until steam blurred the glass. Five feet eight and roughly nine and a half stone. Surely that wasn't too bad?

Jeff used to say she was Junoesque, made her feel proud to be tall and curvaceous. But Suzie Lake had made her feel like an Amazon, and if Suzie was Dan Gather's sort of woman then he obviously preferred chic, fine-boned brunettes.

Oh, blow the man, why should she give a damn if he found her attractive or not?

Because you fancy him! teased a provocative little voice inside her head. That's right, lots of that lovely smelly bath essence Staff Baines gave you. It's been gathering dust on the shelf since last Christmas.

What nonsense, said Ruth sensibly. I just find him interesting, as a person.

Gingerly she sank into the chilly foam, sighing as the hot, silky, perfumed water beneath enveloped and caressed every inch of unresisting flesh . . .

Her eyes closed in bliss. But her thoughts were troubled. What was it the twins had said . . . About Danny Gather seeming to be accident prone? Poor motherless child! No wonder he ran to his father whenever the doctor visited the school. How did the first Mrs Gather die? Why did he have to board when his home was just miles away? Had the doctor's second wife insisted on it? Didn't Beatrice want Danny at home?

Ruth shook her head slowly, perplexed that any father could be so insensitive, so blind to the obvious needs of his son. Her own father had died, when she was eleven, of a heart attack. He had been the best of fathers and his death had been a dreadful blow. Her mother had never married again, but once her daughters were at the comprehensive had gone back to teaching music in primary schools.

And now she, Ruth, had lost Jeff in dreadfully uncertain circumstances, so that on a wave of pain it occurred to her that where the most important men in her life were concerned she too might be considered accident prone. A link between the nurse and the schoolboy . . .

'Eat up, Ruth dear, they won't keep.' Mrs Rogers indicated the buttery scones—baked fresh that morning after early church—topped with strawberry jam and a mouth-watering dollop of rich Devon cream.

'Mum, I've had three already, and after that huge lunch . . . besides, I have to think of my figure!'

It was just a light-hearted throwaway remark, but her mother pounced on it with hopes afresh. Did that mean a new man in Ruth's life? This young sports master, perhaps, who'd been so helpful in settling her in? You never could tell with Ruth. She wasn't a girl to wear her heart or her heartaches on her sleeve.

A teacher husband would be no bad thing, though of course they'd never have much money! Seeing her daughter's face transformed by laughter, Peggy Rogers was mighty relieved. All through that crisis, while they had still been searching, Ruth hadn't—so far as Peggy knew—taken one night off work, concealing her grief beneath her customary calm, professional exterior. Such a brave girl. And of course there'd never been a body, which made everything so much worse.

Ditchingham House, mused Peggy Rogers with satisfaction as she refilled Ruth's teacup, was having the desired effect. She'd never been happy about her daughter working permanent nights at that nursing home. No denying it was a very responsible job for a twenty-six-year-old. And it had fitted in well with Ruth's and Jeff's lifestyle—him away such a lot and Ruth being able to save up her holidays to be with him when he was home on shore leave. Just as well there had never been children! thought Mrs Rogers, stuffing the knitted cosy over the Devon Violets teapot. Jeff had wanted his young wife all to himself. It was sometimes like that when there was such an age difference, and having been alone so long. Mrs Rogers, though she'd liked her sailor son-in-law extremely well, had suspected he'd never really intended to start a family. Still, that had been between him and Ruth. None of her business.

'Penny for them, Mother dear!' teased Ruth, but her mother just smiled and shook her head.

Ruth was asking after Marion, her elder sister, who lived in Kent and with her husband George ran a small garden centre. Marion was having more luck with plants than with babies.

Soon after, she left, so as to get back while there was

still daylight. She didn't like driving in the dark, unpleasantly dazzled by oncoming car lights. Contact lenses might solve the problem . . . she thought she might do something about trying a pair.

As she drove she slotted in a cassette and was soon singing along to a bouncy Country and Western number. She swivelled the volume control and Dolly Parton's voice vibrated through the white Metro. Ruth put her foot down, eager to be back at Ditchingham House, chuckling to herself at the memory of Dan Gather blasting her sitting-room with the Philharmonia at full throttle. It was all too easy to smile *now*, here in the safety of her little car, on the inside lane of the motorway with bigger cars swishing past at ridiculous speeds. Illogically she felt safer here among all this relentless speeding traffic than alone with that man in her own sitting-room!

She hadn't mentioned him today. Her mother was too astute, and Ruth didn't feel able to describe Dr Gather objectively.

Everything would be all right, she reassured herself, her face solemn with certainty, once she got used to working with him . . .

Memories of their initial clash of tempers would fade. She'd be able to form cooler judgements. His physical impact would lessen.

As if to mock her for her innocence, Ruth's inner vision suddenly filled with the height and breadth of Dan Gather. She wanted to stop the car, but yet she must press on, in her nostrils the pungent dampness of his waterproofed coat, her heartbeats racing, her fingers gripping tight to the wheel.

Don't forget this is a man who has sent away his motherless son, brought a new woman into his life and set her before his first wife's children. Insensitive at best, and cruel at the worst. The very opposite of darling, gentle Jeff.

Ruth drove on in silence, her face grave and unsmiling.

An enigmatic man. Easy to dislike ... and yet ... and yet ...

'Oh, *hell*!' complained Sister Ruth Silke out loud. 'Why on earth couldn't the school doctor be your average nice, caring, ordinary family GP?'

A new and disturbing thought struck her.

And what had he done with the beautiful Suzie Lake?

CHAPTER FOUR

RUTH hadn't bargained on a desk job—handwritten records to plough through, letters from parents, bumf from the admin offices. A computer linked to the big one over in the main building would be far more efficient and save this time-wasting messing about with bits of paper.

'We've got customers!' sang out Mrs Downie, sticking her cheerful head round the office door.

Ruth perked up on the instant.

'That's what I like to hear! Wheel 'em in.'

'Oh, these two are ambulant,' joked back Mrs Downie. 'In you go, my dears, Sister Silke won't bite.'

Two overawed pupils who had suddenly lost their tongues at the sight of Ruth in uniform came slowly in. Two pairs of thick-lashed dark eyes examined her with nervous solemnity.

She guessed she did look a bit different in uniform, RCN badges on the lapel of her trim white dress, dressings scissors in her breast pocket, her waist defined by a navy grosgrain belt and her silver nurse's buckle. And a dainty frilled cap where Miss McCarthy's fierce head had worn the starched-linen winged affair of her own long-gone hospital days.

Ruth's skirts were probably a foot shorter too!

'Hello, Danny.'

Ruth smiled, concealing her first reaction of dismay. She must be kindly but not encouraging of social calls.

'What can I do to help?'

Mrs Downie had closed the door behind them and gone back to the ward where she was tidying and rearranging furniture in accordance with Ruth's wishes.

'I've brought Rosie, my little sister, to see you,' Danny said awkwardly, suddenly unsure of their reception. Then, turning to the little girl clinging tightly to his hand, he said in a whispered gabble, 'Go on, Rosie, say hello—she's instead of Matron, I told you. If you feel sick you come over here, see?'

Yes, as she'd suspected, this was a social call. Ruth was grinning inside, they were such an appealing pair; but she kept her face under control, saying gravely, 'Hello, Rosie Gather. This is very nice of you both to come and see me. But do your teachers know where you are?'

One swift glance at their shoes showed that Rosie had been dragged the short cut across the playing-field, and she was breathing heavily as if her brother had tugged her along rather fast for her little red woolly legs. Their cheeks glowed pink from the brisk April air and their eyes shone with expectation. Of what, wondered Ruth . . . a dose of TLC?

'It's all right,' explained Danny earnestly. 'It's break time and Rosie was out to play. Sometimes I go over with my friends and we play Catch with her. She's good fun and can run ever so fast, can't you Rosie? And she never cries when she falls over. We call her "Dangerous" when she wears red tights and red hair ribbons.'

Rosie beamed in delight and displayed charmingly gappy teeth. She fiddled with her untidy plaits and one of the red ribbons came off in her hand.

Ruth held out her arms to the child. 'I'd better fix that for you,' she said gently.

Rosie stood obediently still as Ruth found brush and comb and replaited her hair. Danny balanced on his heels, his hands in his pockets, humming the new tune they were learning in choir. He felt very happy. Pity Dad wasn't here, but he'd see him on Saturday.

'There, now you're all tidy. I do like your dress, Rosie. It's a lovely dark green.'

Rosie found her tongue. ''Tisn't a dress,' she explained, looking up at this tall lady in white, with the pretty face and hair, just as Danny had said. 'It's a pinafore. And I got a jumper underneath.' Up came the skirt to display a bundle of red tights and white vest and jumper around her plump middle.

'Rosie!' reproved her brother, giggling fit to burst.

'You could do with a bit of sorting out, miss,' said Ruth, and proceeded to smooth things out and tuck things in.

'I dress myself,' said Rosie proudly.

Danny was spluttering into his hand; he obviously found his sister a highly entertaining companion. 'You should see what she puts on sometimes,' he volunteered with all the sophistication of the almost-eight-year-old. 'Dad has to make her change sometimes at breakfast. She lives at home and I live at school. She's part time. On Mondays and Wednesdays and Fridays she goes home at quarter past twelve. I used to when I was little.'

'And would you rather be living at home?' asked Ruth carefully.

Danny shrugged his shoulders in a curiously old

manner. 'I don't mind,' he said noncommittally. 'I'd miss my friends if I went home every day. Julian and Andy . . . we have brilliant fun at night. It's nice here.'

'I'm sure you must miss your daddy.'

'Yeah, I do miss my dad. C'mon, Rosie, we better had go.'

Poor little chap. Still . . . he'd end up in hot water if he sneaked out of lessons whenever Dr Gather was on site. Ruth decided to have a quiet word with Danny's housemaster.

'I'll see you again this afternoon. I'm going to come round and talk to all the classes so everybody knows who I am. And now,' she said firmly, not wishing to single the doctor's children out for special attention, nor encourage further impromptu visits, 'I want you both to wipe your shoes on the grass and walk back along the paths.'

They brought their coffee to the office and Mrs Downie sat in the easy chair while Ruth swivelled round from her desk to face her new colleague.

'Isn't Rosie Gather gorgeous? I could just eat her!' enthused Mrs Downie, whose two sons were at the junior school in nearby Tether. 'I love to see little girls with plaits, but it's not the fashion much nowadays. Too much work for busy mums, I should guess.'

An SEN of considerable experience, Carol Downie had joined the centre a year ago to cover nine-till-three during term-time. Ruth was finding this homely, practical woman worth her weight in gold—which was just as well, for the two would be working together every weekday.

'I should have liked a staff meeting, but it's impossible to get my part-time nurses together. How do you feel about the changes I'm suggesting? Be honest with me, I'm not proud, I can take it.'

'I don't think you're going to tread on any toes, Sister. We need some updating round here. It's what Mr Raven and Dr Gather want. You'll get all our support.'

That was fair comment. Miss McCarthy had been a splendid nurse, and St Thomas's trained—one of the famous Nightingale brigade. But Ruth, a modern girl from the Queen Elizabeth in Birmingham, was bursting with ideas of her own. 'I want things to be more child-centred,' she'd explained to Carol Downie as together they'd rearranged the six-bedded ward to make it less like hospital and more like home.

'Miss McCarthy wouldn't approve,' chuckled Mrs Downie. 'I can just imagine what she'd say about her pristine magnolia walls! I'd great respect for her—we all had—but I have to say she terrified *us*, even if Dr Gather could twist her round his little finger. And she made our lives a misery over the hall floor. Kids were scared to come in the place. She had us chasing behind them with a mop. You can't run a sick bay for kids like an intensive care unit! I think the hall looks great—apart from that ruddy floor. I'll go and get the mop.'

Once term was under way Ruth intended to tackle Frank Jolly, the art master, about mounting an artwork exhibition to make the entrance hall more welcoming. 'Whatever next?' she could just hear Miss McCarthy breathing down her neck. In the meantime she had put up vivid posters and filled the wide, sunny window-sills —'They'll be knocking those flying, you mark my words!'—with scarlet and pink potted geraniums begged from the head gardener's greenhouses.

Comics and jigsaw puzzles had been laid out on the corner table where meals were served . . . 'Encouraging malingerers! Extra prep is what these children need, Mrs Silke. Where did you say you trained?'

With a forefinger Ruth probed the damp soil in the pots she'd saved for her office and turned the sturdy plants to face the sunshine they craved, pulling a wry face at the prospect of her formidable predecessor returning for a visit of inspection, poking in every nook and cranny for the ashtrays she'd suspect Ruth of having secreted about the building, the better to indulge her secret addiction when the coast was clear . . .

The sheer awfulness of that day of interviews! Ruth still winced at the memory, yet knowing full well that poor Miss McCarthy would have resented even Florence Nightingale taking her place. Anyway, here I am, in residence, she reminded herself; and the future looks pretty rosy—so long as Dan Gather and I can establish some kind of *modus vivendi*.

The headmaster arrived for a tour of inspection and declared himself well pleased. Just what his pride-and-joy medical centre cried out for: a first-class, energetic, up-to-the-minute nurse running the show.

Charles Raven was one of the new breed of young and vigorous school chiefs, well into modern technology and determined to lead a thriving establishment. His staff tended to be on the young side, which accounted for the number of prams and pregnant wives on the premises. Just as well this quietly attractive girl was unlikely to reproduce in the foreseeable future.

Ruth's request for a computer got the warmest of receptions. 'I shall set the wheels in motion this very day,' he promised, bustling off on his rather short legs and leaving Ruth feeling a bit guilty that she'd harboured a suspicion that Charles was a pompous smoothie . . . Dan Gather was state of the art as far as those qualities were concerned!

At Ruth's elbow the telephone shrilled. 'Sister here,' she answered automatically. 'Ah, the poor thing! Of course. Right away.' The receiver went down with a click. 'Mrs Downie!' she called. 'They've a crisis in St Margaret's—a very tearful new girl whose parents have moved to Brussels. I'm just popping across.'

Today was the first day of term and a bit of an anticlimax after the hectic activities which Ruth understood always surrounded the return of the boarders. Yesterday had been all systems go, an endless procession of cars disgorging trunks and teddy bears, parents to reassure, letters for Sister Silke concerning holiday ills and upsets. Nothing too alarming: one appendix recuperating and requesting Off Games for a fortnight and would Dr Gather keep an eye on Kate as there'd been a small bit of bother with her stitches? Another appendix at the 'grumbling' stage. Several rashes now subsiding and no longer infectious. And a fractured arm, with plaster cast to be removed in due course.

Twelve-year-old Jonathan Simms, one of the high-flyers in the scholarship class, had fallen out of a tree. He had reddish hair and pale freckly skin and his friends had already started scribbling on the grubby plaster cast on his left arm.

Ruth cast a shrewd eye over the tall gangling schoolboy, waiting glumly here in the office while she read his mother's letter. With that arm out of action, he was probably worried about how he was going to cope with written work in the scholarship class, which Ruth had been told was very academic.

'Rescuing the cat, I see. Who came off worse?'

Jonathan responded with a sheepish grin. 'Samson jumped down himself. Think he wondered what I was doing, actually—lying there yelling my head off!'

'It must have been horribly painful,' commiserated Ruth. She tapped the cylinder of chalk and flexed his warm fingers. 'Not left-handed, are you, Jonathan?'

The sympathy was unexpected and the boy's stiff upper lip quivered. Schoolwork, however, was not uppermost in his mind. It was cricket he was brooding over. 'I'm really fed up with this . . . *stupid thing*!' he blurted out, indicating the immobilised arm with an angry toss of his head. 'I was really looking forward to the cricket season this year. But Dad says my muscles won't be up to much. He thinks I may need some physiotherapy.'

The break was healing well and the weeks would speed past. But Ruth could see this was small consolation for the able youngster. She had a suggestion to make. 'Come and see Dr Gather tomorrow, here in the office, and let's find out what he advises. We'll have you bowling again this term . . .OK, Jonathan? Nothing else worrying you?'

'No, no—great! Thanks tons, Sister Silke.' Looking distinctly more cheerful, Jonathan went off to his House, and Ruth found a queue of parents waiting outside her office. As the headmaster had predicted, having a medical centre was proving quite a draw, and some of the parents came in to inspect the new sister in charge as much as the facilities the school could provide.

Several mothers of younger children came to report hay fever symptoms and there were the asthmatics to supervise. Ruth went carefully over case histories with the parents, noting the predisposing factors and making memos of points she must discuss with the school doctor . . .

Who arrived early, on Tuesday afternoon.

Ruth heard his car pull up with a controlled crunch of tyres on gravel. She looked at her watch and smiled approvingly, but her head remained bent over her papers, intent on finishing the sentence she was writing. For a big man he came in panther-quiet, and her pen juddered on the sheet of A4 when from the corner of her eye she saw the reason why.

He was wearing rubber-soled trainers. And *inches* from her right elbow loomed the powerful expanse of the Gather nether limbs, revealed in splendour by the briefest of tennis shorts.

Ruth's heart began to race in the most peculiar fashion. Sudden and unexpected proximity to a big healthy half-clad male in his prime could certainly stress the cardiovascular system!

Annoyance swiftly disguised her momentary loss of equilibrium. Irritation darkened the blue in her eyes to violet. With all that bare flesh on display, it couldn't be work that was uppermost in his mind. He'd dropped in to tell her he'd got other plans.

'Good afternoon, Dr Gather. You look very *sportif*.' Her tone was wry.

Dropping his car keys on the desk, the doctor pulled up a chair alongside. The neck of his shirt gaped wide, revealing the strong column of his throat. It was too early in the year for a suntan, so Ruth guessed his was the sort of smooth olive-toned skin that always looked lightly tanned. His thigh was inches from hers, bulky with muscle and sinew and a copious fuzz of dark curly hair . . . as good as any on the grassy courts of Wimbledon.

'Right then,' said Dan. 'I suggest we start off by working through the list of all those pupils with any kind of medical problems likely to need my attention. We've got,' he said, checking his heavy gold wristwatch, 'we've got exactly an hour and three quarters before I collect Rosie from Pre-prep, drive her home, and head for Peasdowne Place for a knock-up with the tennis pro.'

Ruth raised an eyebrow. Courting display of the snowy-plumed rural medic! So the sexy get-up was for *Suzie's* benefit. 'You're sure you can spare the time? she questioned with cool irony.

'Just about. And since I see you're already making changes around here, why not get one of those coffee machines for the office? Then you can have some ready for when I get here.'

'Any other requests, while you're about it? Want your car waxed?'

'No, but it's kind of you to offer. Coffee will do. Had no time for lunch.'

'Right!' Making no attempt to conceal her exasperation, Ruth jumped to her feet and thrust a pile of papers at him. 'Read through this lot while I'm gone, and here's a pencil if you want to make notes.'

'Black!' she heard his voice call.

She was back in minutes with instant coffee and a plate of digestive biscuits. Shopping for groceries had been bottom on her list of priorities.

'Aren't you having anything?'

'No,' she said.

She looked Dan Gather right in the eye, blue eye to jet-black. 'And how's Suzie Lake getting on?'

Peasdowne Place was a well-known health farm not half a dozen miles away, and, thanks to this philanthropic doctor, Suzie had landed what she'd ecstatically described as 'a plum of a job'. What it had to do with nursing was anybody's guess.

'She's in her element, of course . . . a girl like that.'

He was implying that Suzie's glamorous looks would be wasted in a casualty department.

'Of *course*!' Was he hoping to make her jealous? Must be a big turn-on to have women scrapping over him!

He was watching her closely, as if hoping to find he'd turned her blue eyes green. He'd be so lucky, she vowed, heated on the inside but, with the poise of her years and her experience, able to withstand his speculative stare. There was a peculiar tremor in her fingers as she adjusted her belt, but the feel of the cool metal of her silver buckle—the outward symbol of her professional status—acted like an injection of common sense.

'Good for Suzie.' And how is your dear wife

Beatrice? I'm so looking forward to meeting her . . .

Ruth got up and walked over to unlock the green filing cabinet, her movements deliberate and unhurried, presenting her back as she found and extracted the records for the autumn and winter terms, taking care to slide the drawer to, smoothly and quietly, returning to her seat with the big maroon-covered record book. All the time she was thinking of Suzie . . .

In apparent concentration she was leafing through the handwritten pages . . .If Suzie really was tangling with Dan Gather, then wasn't it a case of exchanging one married man for another? Out of the frying pan and into the fire? As for that poor trusting woman, the second Mrs Gather, who with such loving care had washed and ironed her arrogant husband's pristine tennis whites . . . My heart goes out to you, you trusting, unsuspecting woman.

None of your business at any rate, chided her sensible inner self. Just don't go and complicate matters further by falling in love with the wretch yourself.

'Now, Dr Gather,' she said briskly, 'since you have such a hectic schedule, I suggest we deal with the lists first and the rest will just have to wait.'

Dan gave Ruth's chilly profile a puzzled stare, seeing something he hadn't noticed before, namely that rather charming aquiline nose. What had put that edge of sharpness in her voice? Here he was, bending over backwards to be pleasant, when it would have saved a hell of a lot of trouble if Mac had stayed on to the end of the academic year.

'This is supposed to be my afternoon off, you know,' he said rather plaintively, 'I've done an early surgery and three morning visits.'

'I quite understand,' said Ruth shortly, thumping down a pile of papers under his nose. 'Most of these children will be familiar to you from the two previous terms. Obviously I've got Miss McCarthy's records to go by, but I'd particularly like to discuss with you care of the two diabetics, and Jilly Bennett's epilepsy. And we have a persistent bed-wetter whose problem stems from the fact that her parents are in the throes of divorce. I'd like to take her out of her dormitory and bring her over here to sleep under my supervision. And can you explain to me why a school of two hundred boarders should have so many asthmatics?'

Dan rubbed his jaw. 'In any prep school of this size I think it's fair to say five to ten per cent of the children may experience some mild wheezing. What you've got to bear in mind is . . .'

Some time later came a knock at the office door and Jonathan Simms's freckled face peered doubtfully in at them, having heard the sounds of laughter.

'Er—Sister Silke told me to be here at three,' he said uncertainly, eyeing the doctor's informal attire.

'C'mon in,' encouraged Dan, standing up and flexing his awesome limbs, in high good humour now that he had proved for himself that Ruth Silke, though lacking the ideal of a specialist paediatric qualification—as had all the applicants—was more than up to the job; and that in addition to a high degree of competence she was a physically attractive person—which was very refreshing after her corseted and support-stockinged predecessor. *And* a rather dry sense of humour which was frankly intriguing and suggested hidden and possibly dangerous depths . . .

'What has our demon bowler done to himself, then? I remember you in action last year against the Dragon School. Scared the pants off 'em!'

Ruth, with Jonathan's help, filled in the background and stood by as the doctor examined the arm and checked the pulses, assuring himself that the blood supply was in good order and the fracture was healing normally.

'When can the plaster come off?' The question was pathetically eager.

Dan consulted the big calendar on the wall above the desk. He pursed his lower lip, 'Mmm, let's see—I'd suggest the second week in June, then mobilisation therapy to loosen you up and some ultrasonic treatment for dessert. How does that sound, Sister?'

When the boy had gone, Dr Gather said, 'Well, all in all, I think this has been a useful session for both of us.'

Ruth smilingly agreed. He'd been so easy and pleasant with young Simms; and the omens suggested that their doctor/nurse relationship was going to work pretty well. The ironical thought struck her that it seemed as if a truce was unconsciously called when they stopped regarding each other as members of the opposite sex!

Dan picked up his car keys, ready to be off. 'All work and no play makes Jack a dull boy——'

In Ruth's opinion only a man who considered himself anything *but* would come out with a remark like that! Don't be sexist, dear! chided her inner self. Just say to yourself, he's a doctor, not a man, then everything will be fine.

'You should join me some time,' he suggested.

'I haven't played tennis for years. I shouldn't give you much of a game.'

'There are other games.'

Ruth's eyes flickered away from the amusement in his. Her lips tightened in disapproval: what a smoothie! Still, sooner or later—unless he had skin as thick as an ox—he'd get the message that she didn't play *anything* with married men.

'There's a marvellous heated indoor pool . . . you'd enjoy it.'

'You're going to be late for your daughter, Dr Gather.'

Here was her chance to say she'd met Rosie, and what a sweet little girl and so on. But that would only prolong the conversation and imply that she wished to keep in Dan's good books in spite of her refusal to 'play games'.

'Heaven forbid! she cries. Typical female.'

Now who was being sexist . . .? Ruth pulled a face at Dan's departing back. He turned, and she swiftly adjusted her expression into neutral.

'My daughter told me with great solemnity that you gave a "very important" talk to "her school" yesterday.'

Ruth had to laugh. 'She is a sweetie. They both are.'

'You should hear what they say about *you*,' came the cryptic reply as he strode out of the medical centre.

On the office floor lay his navy sweatshirt, forgotten. Ruth retrieved it and hung it on a peg alongside a lone white lab coat. She considered hopping into her Metro and driving round to the Pre-prep building on the far side of school; but already in the distance she could see the slow line of cars making their way out of the grounds and she knew she would not be in time to catch Dan and Rosie before they left.

Leaving the office, she hesitated, went back inside for a moment and, going to her own quarters, left his sweatshirt on her bed.

CHAPTER FIVE

'SISTER SILKE?'

'Yes, Danny?'

'Can I come on your table, *please*, Sister Silke?'

It was supper and the children could choose where to sit, unlike lunchtime when they had to be with their own class at a regular table. Uniform had been changed for mufti, but jeans were forbidden and sensible clothing was the order of the day.

Danny wore a red and white striped T-shirt, and the baggy school shorts had been swapped for green cotton trousers. He had an old graze above his left elbow and one of his fingernails was black where a door had slammed on it earlier in the week. He'd been across to see Ruth three times in as many days. She was secretly amused by the seriousness with which he presented the smallest scratch for her to dab with iodine, always asking if she thought he should show his father and accepting her gentle shake of the head with a bleak little grin. They both knew he was trying it on. But all the same, the child's obvious need weighed on Ruth's mind. It seemed she was becoming a surrogate parent, and she worried that she should be singled out in this way by this vulnerable child. But she had not the heart to send him away.

Pupils sitting next to the member of staff on each table acted as table monitors, bringing the food to be served and afterwards clearing away. 'How's the finger,

Danny? Can you carry the plates, do you think?'

'Course I can,' said Danny with a beaming grin.

'Right then, off you go, you and Melanie. And be careful now.'

'Yes, miss, I mean, Sister.' Danny went off with Melanie, a giggly little thing with a fair ponytail. The smell of sausages made Ruth's stomach shrivel, but it was favourite school fare—especially with baked beans and grilled tomatoes.

There was a dreadful crash in the direction of the hatch. Heads swivelled, and the chattering stilled. 'Danny Gather!' exclaimed an exasperated voice. 'Just look what you've done!'

With a sigh Ruth laid aside her table napkin and went to investigate. Chips of white crockery lay scattered on the parquet floor and one of the cooks was leaning crossly through the hatch, waving a ladle at the unfortunate Master Gather—whose eyes were welling with tears. Just like his sister Rosie.

Poor chap! thought Ruth, grimacing at this fresh catastrophe. 'He's hurt his hand,' she explained, sending Danny back to the table and herself collecting the tray of sausages and tomatoes and a dish of beans. 'It's my fault: I should have sent another child.'

'He's a walking disaster area, that one,' grumbled the cook, but softened slightly, tut-tutting as she set to work with a broom. 'If ever a kiddie was in the wars, and him with his dad a family doctor. I don't know.'

Next morning, twenty minutes after break, the phone shrilled in the office. Carol Downie took the call.

Ruth was in the ward doing the TPRs for two cases

of tonsillitis and a gastric upset from the scholarship class when Carol came in looking rather bemused, concern wrinkling her brow as she asked if it would be OK for her to go across to the first form and collect an injured pupil.

Danny Gather was in the middle of a French lesson and under adult supervision, but nevertheless he had somehow managed to hurt himself. 'Madame Lavisse is in a bit of a flap. Says the child's swelling up like a football.'

A *football*? To Ruth's sceptical ears that sounded like a bit of mistranslation.

As it turned out, it was a hand injury; and not even the same hand Danny had trapped in the door. One look at the badly grazed skin and swollen red knuckles told Ruth it must be extremely painful. Danny was pulling horrible faces and obviously making a huge effort not to cry.

'How did this happen, Danny?'

In indignant, breathless spurts the sorry tale emerged. Smith-Pryke had *deliberately* dropped his best rubber—one that looked and smelled like a banana—down the back of the radiator beside their desks. Danny had forced his right hand down to get hold of the rubber, which was stuck halfway. His hand had also got stuck. He'd tried to wrench it back up before Madame turned round from writing on the blackboard and had hurt himself so badly he'd yelled aloud in agony, giving the French mistress the most fearful turn.

Very gently Ruth examined the fingers and the squashed knuckles and dressed the oozing graze, supporting the hand in a high sling to help reduce the swelling. 'I don't think anything's broken,' she comforted the child, 'but your father might think it best for you to be X-rayed. You sit here quietly and read a comic while I ring the surgery.'

Danny dropped his 'bravely dying swan' act and perked up. 'Dad'll be out doing visits now,' he said eagerly. 'You'd better ring Auntie Bea.'

'Thank you, Danny, that's most helpful.' Poor child, having to call Mrs Gather Auntie.

Ruth went to the office and dialled.

At first it seemed there was no one in; but finally a woman's voice answered, sounding rather vague as if she had been disturbed from a nap and was feeling sleepy. Perhaps they'd had a late night and Beatrice was having a lie-in. She could scarcely repeat her own telephone number.

Ruth introduced herself.

The woman on the other end sounded a bit dithery for a doctor's wife accustomed to taking calls from anxious patients.

Calmly, so as not to alarm, Ruth explained the situation.

'Oh, dear! Poor little Danny! Not *again*. Oh, dear.' Mrs Gather seemed genuinely upset. 'I—I'll see if I can get Dan on the car phone. I'll tell him to come straight to the school.'

'If he could just call me and confirm——'

But the line was dead. Mrs Gather had already rung off. 'Bother!' said Ruth aloud. Moments later the phone rang again and the dithery voice said, 'Dan's on his way,' and the phone crashed down.

How very odd! How had so formidable a man got

involved with a woman like that? Or had marriage to Dan turned poor Beatrice into a nervous wreck? It wasn't hard to imagine! Small wonder then that Bea didn't feel up to coping full time with a boisterous hyperactive schoolboy.

Even the sight of his beloved father couldn't raise Danny's usual brilliant smile. He winced and whimpered, but did as he was asked, earning a pat on the rumpled head and a 'There's a brave chap!' when the examination was over.

Dan straightened up. 'I'm not sure,' he admitted. 'The reaction we're getting is a bit much. I'm really not happy about it, and to be on the safe side I'd like him checked. Can we get someone to take him along to A & E? His housemaster's wife, perhaps?'

'You take me, Dad!' pleaded Danny, frightened now it seemed he'd done himself some real damage.

'I can't, Danny, I've still got some calls to make.'

'Then I want Silkey to take me. I won't go with anyone else.'

All the staff had nicknames: Sister Silke wasn't likely to escape. Ruth raised an eyebrow, secretly amused.

'Look, son, you've been down there so often you could find your way blindfold.'

Dr Gather picked up the phone and dialled Casualty. 'Can you put me through to Sister ... Yes, it's Dr Gather here from Ditchingham. I've got a child here at the prep school with a hand injury ... a traumatic synovitis. Probably nothing to worry about, but we'd like to be on the safe side. The name's Danny Gather. That's right, my boy ... You and he are old friends?' He scowled at

Danny, who took refuge in his comic. 'Hyperactive? You could say! Many thanks.' Dan thumped down the receiver. 'For God's sake, Danny, you'll be eight soon. Can't you learn to look after yourself? Look at all the trouble you cause!'

The harshness of his words caused Ruth to wince for the child. Her eyes were hostile, but she could tell Dan was too pressed for time to notice; probably he didn't give a fig, either.

'They're expecting him. His name's on the list, so you shouldn't have to wait. OK, Ruth?'

He didn't seem to notice he'd used her first name.

He did at least give his son a warm hug before he rushed away.

Late that afternoon Ruth rang with good news. It was a nasty sprain, but the X-ray showed no bone injury.

'I'm keeping Danny here overnight,' she said curtly.

'I don't see any need for that.'

'Nevertheless, it's been a painful ordeal for him and I don't think he should sleep in his dorm tonight. I know he'd like to see you.'

'No can do. I'm going to a concert in Bath.'

'I see.'

Dan noted the huffy note in Sister Silke's voice. She clearly thought he was a horrible uncaring father who, however busy, should have made time to see his son. He held the phone away from his ear, sighed and shook his head; doctors' families were always the last to get attention. But it was Bea's birthday and his son was in excellent hands.

'That's right, Sister. You dish out the TLC and I'll

drop in tomorrow. Bye.'

That evening Ruth checked through the medical records for evidence. What she found wasn't exactly reassuring. There in Matron's splendid black ink, it was, a whole chapter of accidents, nothing serious, thank goodness, but since his days in the kindergarten class of the Pre-prep department—he must have arrived there not long after his mother's death—Danny had hurt almost every portion of his anatomy.

Hmm, thought Ruth, noting her own entries—the trivial scrapes and grazes, the bruised finger, today's drama: I'm going to have to take up cudgels with his father. How on earth can Dan Gather be so *blind*? And how can a stepmother not love such a dear scruffy little chap who's the *image* of his dad . . .?

Ruth sat drumming her fingers on the desk top, her face solemn and very determined. Well, Bea, whether you like it or not, here is a troubled child who'd be far happier living at home and coming in to Ditchingham House as a day boy. Oh, I daresay I shall get torn off a strip for poking my oar in, but within this school I share the responsibility for every pupil's physical and mental welfare. I just can't sit back and say nothing.

Every Friday after choir practice Danny and his friends hared off to the tuckshop to spend their fifty pence pocket money. Singing was thirsty work, especially on a warm May evening.

'Bottle of pop, please, Mrs Beaks,' panted Danny, hopping on the spot with impatience. He'd got to change out of school uniform before the supper bell.

'Which sort do you want, Danny?'

'Ice-cream soda for me, cherryade for Andrew and beer for Julian. Please.'

'You little tykes,' chuckled Mrs Beaks, handing over a bottle of dandelion and burdock for Julian.

'Hurry up, you guys,' swaggered Andy in a fake American accent. 'the prep bell's gonna go soon.'

'C'mon!' The three sped off for the shrubbery over by the medical centre. A circle of shiny green laurel bushes hid them from view. Running had churned up the gassy drinks, and when Danny unscrewed his bottle cap ice-cream soda fizzed all over his shoes and socks.

'Hey, give us a swig, Gather, you pig! Thought we were gonna share!'

'You'll be sick if you drink all that before supper,' warned Julian, struggling to open his bottle.

'Good! Then I can go and see Silkey.'

'Anyone would think she was your *mum*!'

'Wish she was!'

'I can't get the top off mine,' groaned Julian.

'Give it here, Flight, you couldn't get the top off a flea. Cor, it looks just like real beer. All frothy . . .'

Ruth was going to the cinema in Bath with Angus Stewart—her first evening out for five whole weeks.

She was handing over to the relief nurse.

'Peter in the side ward is feeling pretty miserable, but it seems a straightforward measles and his mother's going to fetch him home tomorrow. Seventy per cent of our children have been vaccinated, so—touch wood—Dr Dan isn't anticipating a measles epidemic.'

The night nurse said fervently heaven forbid, and

people just didn't realise what a dangerous illness measles could be, and if only all mothers realised how important it was to have their children vaccinated then lives would be saved. Roll on the day when measles was eradicated from the list of childhood diseases. Hear, hear! was Ruth's heartfelt reply.

'Rachel's much better today. She's the ten-year-old diabetic in the far bed. She came to us with a bilious attack, couldn't keep food down and couldn't have her insulin. Dr Gather thinks it was just a touch of flu, but because she wasn't getting her normal calorie-controlled intake we've been monitoring her regularly. She's not hypo. BM Stix is 4.5, and urine's negative to sugar . . .

'Henry—er—Sharp is on oral amoxycillin and just needs to be kept comfortable. Little Pru's got a temp of thirty-eight point one degrees so she needs watching. I've got the bedclothes stripped back and the fan on her, and Dr Gather's coming in to see her first thing.'

Ruth glanced at her watch. Angus had suggested an early start so they could grab a pizza before the film.

All of a sudden Ruth didn't want to go!

Her precious charges. It was quite a wrench to leave them.

Ruefully she chided herself for being an idiot. Mary Spurling was a darned good nurse who had staffed on a paediatrics ward before she'd got married.

'If you have any problems,' she said finally, 'Dr Gather's number is right by the telephone in the office. You will call him, won't you, if you're at all worried?'

'Don't you fret yourself, Sister. You enjoy your evening out. It's a fantastic film, and Robert de Niro's brilliant as usual.'

'And you've been coming here for two years and know the ropes as well as I do, bless you!' smiled Ruth. Perhaps I'm getting *too* attached to this job, kidding myself I'm indispensable!

She went out on to the stone step, standing in the open doorway, taking in great lungfuls of the sweet country air. The groundsmen must have mowed the cricket pitches, for she could smell newly cut grass. Sparrows chattered in the tall silver birches. Distantly a bell clanged its summons and a small green van turned into the parking area bringing over the suppers for the medical centre.

Ruth had fifteen minutes to wash and change. No need for thermals tonight!

Humming softly to herself, she rummaged through her wardrobe. '"Ne'er cast a clout till May is out",' she quoted, blithely heedless of old wives' warnings as she stepped into a gentian blue shirtwaister, buttoning the white buttons, rolling the sleeves way up over her smooth round arms, and fastening a white elasticated belt that nipped in her waist to Victorian proportions. Angus wasn't much taller than she, so tactfully she put on white ballerina-style flats. She mascaraed her lashes navy-blue and was just blotting her pouting rose-pink lips on a tissue when an urgent knocking and cries of 'Sister, come quickly!' brought her dashing to the entrance hall.

It hadn't rained all week. But the three boys were soaking wet. Nurse Spurling was bending over one of the children, her hands cupping his face, tipping back his head. Ruth's heart did a somersault as she saw it was

Danny Gather. And his regular partners in crime, Julian Flight and Andy Pardoe.

'What happened?' she asked sharply, spotting no obviously dramatic injuries.

'These two are just in a sticky mess and Julian has a few splinters in his right hand. Danny seems to have come off the worst, but I can't see anything wrong with his face, so it's mainly his hands and his legs. You might have been blinded, you young scamp! Shaking pop bottles, they were, and one exploded.'

'Andy and I never,' protested Julian.

'It just fizzed itself. From when we were running.'

This was not the moment to be apportioning blame. Ruth blessed those baggy grey cord shorts which had taken the brunt and were full of glass shards, as were the thick grey socks. The rest were embedded in the six inches of sturdy leg that filled the gap.

'Right,' said Ruth, taking charge of the situation. 'Danny, go to the treatment-room. You two, clothes off and into the bath.'

At that moment in came Angus, looking very smart in a silk cravat and a pale linen jacket.

''Ello, 'ello, 'ello! What's going on here?'

Later Ruth awarded him full marks for gallantry in the face of a ruined evening out.

For Angus took off his jacket, rolled up his sleeves, phoned over to St George's House and St Philip's, organised clean clothes and supervised baths, and sat Danny on his lap while Ruth put a pair of headphones on the child's head so as to distract him with pop music while with dissecting forceps and limitless patience she tweezed out each and every splinter, laying the pieces out on gauze for Danny to marvel at—'All that lot inside me!'—then doused his wounds with chlorhexidine before, finally, bandaging them.

'There. All finished.'

She straightened, rubbing the small of her back, threw her disposable gloves into the bin and took off her glasses. There was a small red mark across the bridge of her nose.

'Well, Danny,' she said brightly, 'I'm proud to announce that you've earned yourself one of my special medals!' On his chest she stuck a paper disc with 'Award for Bravery' on it in bold black letters. 'And to celebrate I suggest I cook supper for you and Mr Stewart in my kitchen. There's egg and chips or chips and egg. Which would you prefer?'

They all managed a laugh at this. Which was more than Dr Gather did when *he* heard the sorry tale.

'Can I sleep in the centre tonight?' Danny had begged.

And so his father, arriving early, well before his nine o'clock surgery, found him with his medal on his pyjama jacket, clumsily spooning up porridge with bandaged hands.

'Hell's teeth, Sister, does this child *live* here?'

That was pretty rich, coming from an absentee father! Ruth drew breath, but before she could phrase a suitably cutting remark Dan had hauled up his son by the shoulder and was propelling him along the corridor to the treatment-room, where Ruth's pristine bandaging was swiftly removed and cast aside. Gently cradling the small battered hands in his, the doctor scrutinised the many tiny cuts, which were clean and healthy-looking—thanks to Ruth's meticulous expertise.

'Thought you'd burned yourself,' grunted Dan, his shoulders slumped in so uncharacteristic and weary a way that Ruth, looking down on father and son, was suddenly very moved. 'Tell me what happened.'

Danny did so, and with such innocent candour that it was obviously an accident, without malice aforethought. He pulled up his pyjama legs and displayed bandaged knees. 'You've had a very lucky escape,' said his father. 'Just think if that glass had gone in your eyes! Promise me you'll never shake up pop bottles again.'

'Oh, I didn't, Dad. We ran and it must have got fizzed up. Mr Stewart and me had supper in Silkey's flat because they were going to the pictures and then they couldn't in the end. Silkey had this lovely blue dress and lipstick and everything. She looked really beautiful—like Madonna.'

Ruth was fussing over the dressing trolley, biting the side of her mouth to stop herself from laughing. 'Danny,' she said, 'let me put your bandages back on and then I'll help you with your uniform.'

'I'll see to that,' said a voice from the door, and there was Carol Downie, early as usual. 'Morning, Sister—morning, Dr Gather. You come with me, Danny, and tell me how you got your war wounds. Is he going into school today, Sister?'

'He most certainly is,' growled the doctor. Danny lifted his face for a kiss and left after bestowing on Ruth one of his most angelic smiles.

'Wretched child!' muttered Dan.

'How can you say that? It wasn't his fault.'

He eyed her sceptically. 'And how do you make that out?'

Ruth tossed her head and the frills on her cap shivered. 'I blame the manufacturer. In fact, I'm seriously thinking of ringing the managing director and making a formal complaint. If there was a flaw in the glass and if the bottle wasn't filled right to the top——'

'Rubbish! Danny's downright naughty, that's the root of it all.'

Ruth dashed a hand across her forehead. It was now or never. The poor boy seemed to have no champion but her.

'The root of it all, Dr Gather,' she said, willing her voice not to quiver, 'is that your son needs to be at home experiencing a proper family life. The root of it all,' she repeated for emphasis, 'is that he misses *you*. He's accident prone because he thinks no one really cares what happens to him.'

Dan rolled his eyes to the ceiling. 'Rubbish! I never heard such naïve and sentimental psychology! You've been reading too many women's magazines.'

He wasn't going to take her seriously. It quite took the wind out of her sails. She'd expected scorn, fury, to be told to mind her own business. Anything but this mild, amused derision. Blast the man!

Well, here was a truth he couldn't argue with. 'Had Danny gone home after choir practice, none of this would have happened,' she pointed out coldly.

'And your night out,' he had the gall to say, 'wouldn't have been screwed up. Yes, it must have cramped Stewart's style having Danny hanging around your flat.

No wonder you're so uptight today!'

Angus with Danny on his knee. Angus mopping the tears with his clean hanky. Angus making them both laugh in spite of everything with his dreadful puns and awful jokes . . .

Angus kissing her goodnight and Ruth feeling absolutely nothing and hoping he'd never try that again.

It was all too much, and she stepped forward, her jaw set and her eyes deepening to purple, the pupils mere pinpricks. She was about to do something she would surely live to regret, but oh, the moment of satisfaction!

With her whole force she drew back her arm to slap Dan's face.

But he must have seen it coming, for his foot kicked back and slammed the door shut, giving them privacy, and his left hand caught her wrist just inches from its target.

'Ruth, calm down, I never suspected you could be so emotional,' he murmured soothingly. Not letting go, he pulled her up against him with a strength that made her gasp, her nose on a level with a spotted tie of pale yellow silk, her eyes glued to that fascinating mouth which was deliberately seeking to charm away all her hostility. The crisp blue stripes of his shirt mesmerised her into brief submission. His skin smelled subtly of cologne, slightly spicy, intoxicating . . .

'I appreciate your special interest in my son. But you've seen for yourself that Ditchingham House really is a happy and caring school. You're already making a valuable contribution, but you must concede that I have much more experience of children than you do. Some seven-year-old boys do tend to be accident prone, especially if they're vigorous and healthy and highly active. But the answer isn't to wrap them in cotton wool. Believe me, I understand my son. I was just like him at that age—always in trouble, always hurting myself. And look at me, I've survived.'

Certain that he had softened her up a bit, he slackened his grip, and Ruth took her chance and wrenched herself free. She wheeled away and turned to face him, furious with him, with herself, with the whole darned disastrous day.

'It's my job to concern myself with *all* the children's welfare. It is unfortunate but purely coincidental that Danny is *your* son. I'm convinced he would benefit from being a day boy and I would be shirking my responsibilities if I didn't tell you so, regardless of who you happen to be. If you choose to ignore my professional advice, then that's entirely up to you. But don't accuse me of being emotional!'

'Look,' said Dan, his voice so reasonable, humouring her, 'it's just not practical for Danny to be a day boy. He'd be bored stiff without his friends. Danny adores Bea, and Bea adores him, but I can't expect her to devote herself entirely to my children. Let's face it, most of the day she's on another planet.'

This was the most incredible nonsense Ruth had ever heard. She listened, utterly speechless. What sort of tyrant was this Beatrice? And by what magic had she managed to enslave a devastating man like Dan Gather?

'She's longing to meet you; keeps saying we must invite you to supper. But be warned, she's a diabolical cook. Rosie and I only survive because we've got cast-iron digestions and Marks and Spencer to fall back on. Damn! I'm late for surgery.'

With Dan gone, Ruth slumped against the treatment couch, her legs trembling and her brain awhirl. She'd been made to seem a fool, blandly warned about getting over-interested in his son. What did he take her for? she puzzled . . .

The truth dawned with an awful clarity. Obviously he took her for the sort of woman who'd try to worm her way into his good books via Danny. Just another with a crush on him, who needed a smooth, practised rebuff to keep her in her place. Perhaps he thought she was——

The telephone interrupted and demanded her attention and, frowning, Ruth lifted the receiver. 'Hold on,' she said, 'I'll just check the diary. Yes, Marcus does have an ENT appointment tomorrow. I'll be taking him down myself. Two-thirty—that's right.'

CHAPTER SIX

MORNING SERVICE ended, and with the organ thundering the Widor Toccata the whole school filed out of chapel in their Sunday-best uniforms, emerging into the eye-blinking Whitsun sunshine. Teachers in flowing black academic gowns now relaxed their strict supervision and the orderly ranks broke into excited chatter, rushing to greet their parents who were shaking hands first with the chaplain, the Vicar of Ditchingham, and then with the headmaster and his staff.

In the vestry, twenty-four boy choristers, the chosen few, were disrobing, angels no longer as they unclipped white ruffs from itchy necks and pulled cotton surplices over their heads, ruffling neatly combed hair. Impatient fingers tackled the many small buttons of their long red cassocks, for most were eager to jump in the family cars and head for home and the half-term holidays. Danny watched what the others did, unbuttoned his own just enough to step out of, and hurriedly stuck it on a coat-hanger. 'Take your surplices home for laundering,' reminded the junior music master. 'And well done, chaps—the anthem was perfect. All our hard work was worthwhile. Have a good holiday!'

Not everyone was going home. Ruth and Angus with several other younger staff had volunteered to supervise the thirty or so boarders obliged to spend the holiday week at Ditchingham House because their parents were working abroad.

Danny dashed past, his white surplice rolled up in a ball and crammed under his arm as he headed for a maroon Volvo estate parked outside St Philip's House. Ruth reached out and grabbed him by the shoulder. 'Not so fast, young man. That's not your father's car.'

'Dad's on call. I've got a lift home with Tom Hadleigh.'

'Does your housemaster know? He does; fair enough. Congratulations, by the way, on getting your robes. You must be the youngest in the choir.'

'I am!' said Danny proudly, waiting with breathless good manners to be dismissed.

'Off you go, then.' And what a pity, she mused—'Whoops, careful!' as Danny almost tripped over the dangling surplice in his headlong rush to join his friend—what a pity your family couldn't spare the time to come and see their rough-tough youngster turn into an angel!

Danny and Rosie and Dr Gather were spending the week at a cottage nestling on a remote hillside in Wales. Without Beatrice. Beatrice had apparently gone off somewhere on her own.

With a shrug, Ruth reminded herself for the *nth* time that the Gathers' unorthodox family life was none of her business!

Danny—touch wood—had been accident free since the pop bottle drama. And their difference of opinion over the boy had not been referred to since. Nurse and doctor were getting on reasonably well; but Ruth was taking no chances, at all times treating Dan with polite and formal respect. He might neglect his own children, but where the school was concerned he was a tower of strength. In fact he'd made it quite clear that she was always to call him out if she was the least bit worried, whatever the hour, day or night, about any child. To know this was immensely reassuring.

'Penny for your thoughts.' The chaplain joined her and clasped her hand between his as if she were one of the younger mums.

'Half-term already,' smiled Ruth. 'I was telling myself I can hardly believe it.'

'You've settled in so well we feel you've been here for years. Confidentially,' said Kenneth Richardson, drawing her aside and out of earshot but still grasping her hand, 'I'm delighted you and Dan Gather have struck up such a rapport. We had our fears on the governing body that you might not enjoy working with him. But you look so bright and beautiful, and you seem so happy——'

Ruth submitted to being led along, somewhat embarrassed by what she was hearing.

Jonathan Simms came up to say goodbye, his fracture almost healed, to be congratulated by the chaplain. 'Young man, you read the lesson splendidly. Now enjoy your half-term.'

'And when you come back,' promised Ruth, 'we'll get the exercises going and have you playing cricket by July.'

Simms made for his parents' Jaguar and the chaplain resumed their tête-à-tête.

'Dan's had a difficult time these past few years, as perhaps you know.' Haven't we all? was Ruth's ironic but silent response. 'It would have been easy to rub him up the wrong way, but you're a very calm, soothing girl, and that's much appreciated here.'

Spare my blushes! thought the 'calm' girl, feeling rather silly standing there holding hands with the kindly priest - who hadn't finished yet. 'Beatrice does her best, but it's unfair really to expect her to cope with everything on top of her own work.'

'Oh, really?' Ruth gave him a puzzled questioning look, but just then the headmaster detached himself from a circle of parents and strode purposefully in their direction, his gown billowing behind. He grabbed the Vicar of Ditchingham by the elbow. 'Sorry to drag you away, Ken, but I want you to meet the Williamson parents. He's got a difficult London parish . . . Getting on OK with the computer, Ruth?'

'Fine!' Ruth was looking forward to an empty sick bay and the chance to get the medical records on to floppy disc. The two men walked away, the tall, gaunt priest in his shabby black cassock and the short vigorous headmaster in his ermine-trimmed Oxford hood and gown. 'A considerable asset . . . don't know what we'd do without her!' floated back to Ruth, and feeling she was so little stretched here in this very pleasant place she lowered her blushing head.

In no time at all a bunch of children surrounded her. 'We're going swimming!' they cried out joyously. 'Sir says we've to ask you very nicely if you'll come and watch us. So will you *please*, Sister Silke?'

'Is Mr Stewart going in the water with you?'

'Yes, Sister.'

'Then I'd love to come and watch.'

'What a pity our half-terms didn't coincide,' her mother

had written. 'Never mind, perhaps we can go away together in the summer. The Lake District would be nice. Marion and George are well and send their love. No luck yet with the baby.'

There was a postcard too, a glossy photograph of what looked like a stately home. Ruth turned it over and was surprised and very pleased to find the unfamiliar large black handwriting belonged to Suzie Lake, of all people. 'This is just the most fabulous job!!! When you get a day off, you must come and see me here. I'll use my influence and get you fixed up with the Treatment. You won't recognise yourself afterwards, and that's a promise! Here's my number. Give me a ring. PS. I've been seeing quite a bit of Devastating Dan. And isn't he just!!'

Ruth raised her eyebrows at all those exclamation marks and wondered if Suzie realised all the post went to the school office where it was sorted and re-delivered. Devastating Dan indeed! Just so long as no one started rumours that he was devastating Sister Silke! Still, she might well take up Suzie's generous invitation, just to give herself a break from the school routine. If she could get a decent haircut there it would be a big help—her hair was below her collar, and Ruth found that very irritating.

'Saturday night, then. Shall we say seven-thirty? I know Beatrice doesn't like to eat too late.'

'That's very kind of you,' Ruth murmured, and put down the phone. So at last she was to get to meet Beatrice Gather. Complete with zimmer frame, from the sound of it. No wonder Dan had been so stroppy after a wet week in the Welsh mountains with two fed-up children!

They'd met by accident in the grounds when he was visiting Mrs Wrigglesby. Ruth had just popped along with a present for the new baby, but seeing the silver BMW parked outside St Philip's House had decided to turn back when the doctor himself hailed her. She'd enquired about the baby and said she hoped they'd had an enjoyable half-term break, and Dan had growled never again, he could have throttled Danny, and Rosie was the most cussed child on the face of the earth. The weather had been lousy.

'I can't understand it,' said Ruth. 'We've had such a sunny week here.'

'Always sunny where you're around, isn't it, Sister?' he'd jeered. 'Pity I didn't think to invite you along to cheer us all up.'

'Pity you didn't,' responded Ruth calmly, refusing to rise to his bait. 'At least I could have provided more than scrambled eggs and baked beans. Though come to think of it, I've hardly cooked . . . since . . .' Her voice trailed away into a troubled silence. She'd been going to say, 'since Jeff died,' and her hesitation had been from guilty surprise that he was no longer at the forefront of her thoughts. Time heals, her mother had consoled, wise from experience. But to Ruth it had seemed such a cliché . . . so glib. And *then* she hadn't wanted to forget, to be healed.

Little escaped the perceptive Dr Gather. 'Since?' he prompted, his eyes narrowing expectantly as he perceived the crack in Sister Silke's habitual composure.

But Ruth hardly heard him. Faces, voices, crowding in on her imagination. Jeff. Her father. Dan's first wife. Hastily she improvised, a small shake of her head seeming to dismiss her memories. 'Oh—I—er—since I've been eating in the dining-room here in school.'

The tissue-paper parcel in her hands tore under twisting fingers that seemed to belong to some clumsy emotional stranger, and she stared blindly down at the thing she was holding, the matinée jacket crocheted in the evenings when she sat quietly beside the beds of sick children. It had a delicate shell pattern in finest white baby wool, and was the sort of garment she would never, she realised in despair, need to make for herself.

'I—I'm sorry, I have to . . .'

And turning her head away to hide her obvious distress, she forced her tense limbs to take action and almost fled along the paths and through the shrubbery and back to the safety of the empty medical centre.

Motionless for several minutes, Dan Gather stared after her.

He deliberated whether to call and see if Ruth was all right after this extraordinary display . . . one moment her normal self, the next shuddering with some inexplicable emotion.

Was it something he'd said? Jiggling the car keys in his pocket, Dan cast his mind back. An apparently innocent conversation about his holiday . . .

What if he *had* invited her along? Danny would have been over the moon. How that child idolised her! But then it wasn't exactly the done thing to take an attractive young woman you weren't married to to a remote Welsh hillside. That was inviting gossip, and hadn't he had enough of that to last him a lifetime? People meant very well, but even Beatrice got fed up with the flights of imagination which linked him with any unattached female whose face wouldn't frighten the horses . . .

So Ruth had stayed on here at school instead of taking the chance of a half-term break from the stresses and strains of a new job in an unfamiliar environment. Dan shrugged his broad shoulders. Perhaps she had nowhere else to go.

Broodily he scratched the side of his jaw, indecision foreign to his nature. Should he? Yes, he damn well should! That young woman hadn't had twenty-four hours away from this place since term began back in April. And she had thrown herself so wholeheartedly into the life of the school that it hadn't occurred to any of them that she might have problems of her own. They'd all been so very polite, none of them referring to the circumstances by which she came to be alone.

Dan's mind was made up. He'd go over to the medical centre and give her a good talking to about overdoing things.

The car phone shrilled its interruption and Dan cursed aloud. Of all the blasted inventions!

In the silence Ruth lay sobbing bitterly, the tissue-wrapped parcel crushed beneath her on the duvet, her left hand flung out with fingers outstretched to touch all she had left of her husband, a bearded face in a photograph.

It was a fine June evening and the guests had gathered for pre-dinner drinks in the headmaster's rose garden. Some of the species roses were already flowering; their scent hung upon the still air, saturating it with a sweetness that was almost overpowering.

Ruth felt nervous. She told herself this was ridiculous, and took slow deep breaths to fill her lungs with pure clean air. But common sense seemed to have abandoned her tonight, and that air was pure perfume which did nothing to soothe her heaving breast.

All this emotional havoc just because she was going to have to face Dan after that display of weakness the other night. Knowing him, she thought cynically, he'll have diagnosed a straightforward case of PMT! For what was she to Dan Gather other than a generally sensible and down-to-earth nurse, apparently experiencing a one-off episode of biological disturbance? Well, let him think that! Keep the minefield of her emotions a secret, gradually to be detonated when she was alone in bed and cushioned by the solitary dark.

Ruth raised her glass to her lips and gulped thirstily at the chilled white wine.

She knew everyone here. There was no reason to feel anything but comfortable in this friendly company. The head of music who played the chapel organ quite brilliantly and had a penchant for velvet jackets in shades of claret or bottle green, escorting Philippa, his young auburn-haired wife, herself a professional singer and often away on tour with an opera company. Kenneth Richardson in clerical stock and collar and his summer jacket of beige linen. Gwyneth Raven who had swapped her tweeds and silks for colourful Liberty cottons and was right this moment affectionately pulling her husband's leg about his passion for computers.

All of them waiting patiently for the Gathers, who were twenty minutes late.

Ruth's second glass was almost empty. Although her hand was quite steady now, her head was in a whirl.

She couldn't help but smile at being partnered with the tall, lean, stoop-backed Kenneth Richardson—a good thirty years older than she and a father-figure if ever there was one. Thank goodness, she mused muzzily, that they hadn't paired her up with Angus. She'd had quite enough of *his* company over half-term. He'd been eager to get her into a bikini and the swimming-pool, and Ruth had been obliged to confess that she couldn't swim.

But she'd kept quiet about her phobia of deep water.

Suzie had told that shocking tale about Dan Gather throwing two sparring admirers into a pool to cool off, and the way Ruth felt about water, and the way she felt about Dan, were getting inextricably mixed.

A small pulse began to throb at the base of her throat. She found herself wishing like hell she could swim—it was a weak spot, and weak spots must be overcome. Besides, staff and their families had the use of the pool during the holidays, and it was in such a glorious setting surrounded by green lawns and flower-beds, so it would be rather a pity not to be able to take advantage of it.

And—Ruth giggled tipsily into her glass—positively dangerous if Dan was around and she felt like fighting over him.

A lilting Welsh voice broke into her reverie, and with a start she realised her hostess had joined her, her footsteps silent on the grass.

'What a very pretty frock, Ruth. Did you buy it in

Take 4 Medical Romances

Mills & Boon Medical Romances capture the excitement, intrigue and emotion of the busy medical world. A world often interrupted by love and romance...

We will send you 4 BRAND NEW MEDICAL ROMANCES absolutely FREE plus a cuddly teddy bear and a surprise mystery gift, as your introduction to this superb series.

At the same time we'll reserve a subscription for you to our Reader Service. Every two months you could receive the 6 latest Medical Romances delivered direct to your door POST AND PACKING FREE, plus a free Newsletter packed with competitions, author news and much, much more.

What's more there's no obligation, you can cancel or suspend your subscription at any time. So you've nothing to lose and a whole world of romance to gain!

FREE

FILL IN THE FREE BOOKS COUPON OVERLEAF

Your Free Gifts!

We'll send you this cute little tan and white teddy bear plus a surprise gift when you return this card. So don't delay.

Reader Service
FREEPOST
PO Box 236
Croydon
Surrey
CR9 9EL

FREE BOOKS CERTIFICATE

YES please send me my 4 FREE Medical Romances, together with my Teddy and mystery gift. Please also reserve a special Reader Service subscription for me. If I decide to subscribe, I shall receive 6 new books every two months for just £8.10, post and packaging free. If I decide not to subscribe, I shall write to you within 10 days. The free books and gifts will be mine to keep in any case.

I understand that I am under no obligation whatsoever – I can cancel or suspend my subscription at any time simply by writing to you.
I am over 18 years of age.

EXTRA BONUS

We all love surprises, so as well as the FREE books and Teddy, here's an intriguing mystery gift especially for you. No clues - send off today!

1AOD

Mrs/Miss/Ms _____
(Block capitals please)

Address _____

_____

_____ Postcode _____

Signature _____

Bath?'

'Well, actually, I've not yet been into Bath. This came from Monsoon two years back. Jeff chose it——' Ruth said without thinking.

'Ah,' said Gwyneth, tactfully spotting the wavering smile and making a mental note to invite Ruth over for a private chat. One didn't wish to be nosy, but lack of interest was just as bad, and she'd hate this very sweet girl to think no one here cared. She and Charles had wondered about Ruth's personal circumstances—he'd said at interview that she was a widow—but intuitively Gwyneth had felt the first move should come from Ruth herself. And this was the first time she had mentioned her dead husband.

'Such lovely floaty fabric,' enthused Gwyneth. 'And those soft blues and lavenders suit you so well. Mind your skirt on the rose thorns.'

The tenderest breath of a breeze trembled the petals of a newly opened rosebud near Ruth's cheek and her left hand strayed up to stroke its velvety perfection. 'They're here at last!' trumpeted Charles from the veranda, making Ruth's troubled heart start to hammer.

'Isn't she a beauty?' the headmaster's wife was enthusing. 'That glorious shade of apricot. Her name's Maigold.' Funny, thought Ruth a touch woozily, I thought she was called Beatrice! Still, I guessed right about the beauty, didn't I?

'And not only is she rampant, she smells absolutely wonderful too——'

Ruth's eyes rolled in absolute agreement. Well, she would . . .

'But be careful if you sniff her, because she's got

absolutely deadly prickles. Now do come and say hello
to Bea.' Be-ya, was the way Mrs Raven pronounced it,
and that seemed to Ruth quite a good idea as she wasn't
sure she could get her tongue round Beatrish. Following
on wobbly high heels in Gwyneth's charging wake,
Ruth heard rather than witnessed the voluble exchange
of greetings.

'Be-ya darling, late as usual. No, don't worry, I
always allow for it. Now in the garden there's someone
you've been anxious to meet . . .'

CHAPTER SEVEN

'ACCORDING to Dan they've packaged Marilyn Monroe and Florence Nightingale in one young woman named Ruth Silke, and I'm *dying* to meet her!'

It *was* the voice on the telephone; but no longer hesitant or uncertain. And what it was saying was embarrassing enough to turn the mildly inebriated nurse stone-cold sober and stop her right in her wavering tracks.

Seconds later out on to the veranda stepped in person Dan's sophisticated and intimidating partner. Ruth's jaw was in danger of collapse. She caught her lower lip between her teeth. Wrong on so many counts, she felt the evening was turning into a farce. For starters, Beatrice was a good ten years *older* than the doctor.

Her face was pleasant and motherly and her short figure on the plump side. And she wasn't very tall in her cream tussore blouse with a nice cameo brooch at the neck and her long black evening skirt. Her hair was styled in a neat grey perm. And a very puzzled Ruth realised she'd seen Beatrice somewhere before. In fact, she'd got a picture of this woman in her sitting-room!

Feeling confused and extremely foolish, Ruth was thus introduced to Dr Gather's elder sister, who grasped both her hands and kissed her warmly on the cheek, which she could do because she wasn't wearing any lipstick. Everyone else just kissed the air by each other's faces. Dan came strolling in, glanced briefly in their direction and, with no apparent desire to join in the kissing, walked straight over to the drinks trolley, perfectly at home in the Raven's drawing-room, and poured himself a disgracefully huge whisky.

'Danny calls you Silkey, dear girl,' Bea was confiding. 'Apparently they all do in his form. It must be your lovely soft hair.' No one else was in earshot at this precise moment, and Ruth was truly thankful. Her smile felt stiff and false. She could think of nothing to say to Beatrice Gather, who was chatting on entirely unaware that she was personally something of a bombshell and the school nurse was in a mild state of shock. 'I've seen you in the grounds when I've been collecting Rosie, but I'm always late and in too much of a rush to stop. Mostly our kind neighbours bring her home for me when I'm working.'

Ah! Ruth knew who she was now. It wasn't a sight you forgot—one of the collecting grannies—so she'd thought—bouncing her red MGB over the 'sleeping policemen' which were intended to slow down all traffic within the grounds. Her face relaxed into its usual softness and she began to smile for real. This was Dan's *sister*, and a genuinely warm person, with a robust turn of phrase for a lady of mature years.

Dan was watching them now from across the room. He caught Ruth's eye and mockingly raised his glass at her. She acknowledged it with a nod and a coolly arched left eyebrow—this had taken hours in front of a mirror some ten years back and was a gesture saved for occasions when Ruth wanted to appear set on the outside if jelly within. Marilyn Monroe indeed! He was fond of his little jokes. What he meant was she was a hefty piece of nurse. Oh, my lord, sighed Ruth behind her façade of apparent calm. I was too proud to show my curiosity. Well, serves me right. There *is* no second Mrs Gather. And Bea goes out to work—I bet she's a medical social worker—so that's why poor Danny, accident prone or not, has to be a boarder.

Someone pressed more wine upon her and a very preoccupied Ruth raised her glass to her lips, forgetting she had already decided that with her light head she had had quite enough to drink before dinner. Charles claimed the doctor's attention, and with Philippa coming over to kiss Beatrice Ruth could make her own surreptitious appraisal.

This was Dr Gather in a different light. Free to pursue Suzie Lake or anyone else if he so desired.

I should be so lucky, sighed Ruth to herself, her inhibitions dissolved by the fruit of the vine and the heady discovery of the night. She opened her blue eyes wide, permitted those same eyes to rove unblinkered. And what they saw . . . eating was going to be out of the question if she couldn't make herself relax! . . . caused her throat to tighten in the most alarming way. Huge dark pupils stroked the expensively tailored cream linen jacket, memorised the sleek bulk of the body inside that crisp white shirt tantalisingly closed at the throat with a bow-tie of Paisley silk . . . remembered only too well what was inside those sleek black trousers . . .

With a pang Ruth saw that Philippa was aware of him too; that her beautiful hazel eyes glanced his way again and again as if unable to help themselves.

She felt indignant, as if the other woman were trespassing.

The vicar approached with a tall glass of frosty

orange juice which he handed without comment to Beatrice. 'Dear Ken,' she beamed, 'just what the doctor ordered.' She raised her glass of orange juice and said, 'Cheers, everybody!'

People gathered round as if she were some kind of magnet.

'You haven't been working today, have you?' questioned Gwyneth reverently.

'I know it's a cheek, Beatrice, when you're supposed to be enjoying yourself,' pleaded Philippa, her pale face flushing as if she were speaking to royalty. 'But if I pop across and fetch your latest, will you sign it for me?'

'She loves signing books,' grunted Dan from the other side of the room.

'I love signing books!' laughed Bea. 'If you'll return the compliment and sing an aria for me later, Philippa. Yes, of course I've been working. A writer has this need to commit words to paper every day.'

'I don't know how you do it, *and* run Dan and his family as well——'

'I don't know how she does it either,' interrupted a voice that came from behind and above Ruth so that she could feel his warm breath skim the crown of her head. 'But I'm very glad she does do it, I can tell you. I'd be up the creek without a paddle if she didn't.'

His hands rested lightly on her shoulders. 'Look at her!' he murmured in Ruth's ear, full of quiet pride in his sister's achievement. 'Every inch a stalwart of the WI, wouldn't you say? Yet my dear old Bea is one of the world's raciest writers of psychological thrillers. And never wrote a word till she was forty.'

'What did she do before that?' wondered Ruth.

'Oh, medical social work,' said Dan, and wondered why Ruth smiled.

In rushed Philippa with her Penguin paperback of *Deadly Desires* by O.B. Fairfax. The hands removed themselves from her shoulders and Ruth looked quickly up at Dan, receiving a slanting ironic grin that might have been meant for her or Bea.

'Let's stand well back before we get trampled by the fans!'

Turning on his heel, he began to stroll down the garden with the clear expectancy that she would accompany him. Which she did.

On the far side of the shadowy rose arch he stopped and thrust his hands into his pockets, inspecting her with a frank admiration that pinked up Ruth's fine and delicate skin.

She knew it was silly, really, considering her height and unsylphlike shape. But somehow she always felt a bit—well, delicate and feminine in the Monsoon dress. Jeff's choice and Jeff's favourite. And now she was wearing it for another man who was surveying her with unconcealed pleasure.

'Nice frock, Sister Silke. Matches your big blue eyes,' he said, peering amiably down her low neckline and thinking to himself it made a pleasant change from buttoned-up uniform and her reading specs and that rather —um—small pair of jeans. Not a girl with her mind on clothes, he'd concluded on the day of the interview; and he reckoned he'd been right, for as a rule Sister Silke didn't dress to enhance. But then she didn't need to.

'I don't often get to see you dressed to slay.'

Ruth giggled in spite of herself. It was a heady mix, Dan's admiration and Charles's delicious wine. Funny how when you weren't used to it a small glassful could make you feel so happy. 'What about my immaculate turn-out on interview day?' she pouted flirtatiously, a teasing sparkle in her eyes. 'Sabotaged,' she reminded him, 'by your rogue of a son!'

Dan grinned broadly and raised an incredulous eyebrow, recalling that the first emotion Ruth had aroused in him had been a pure cold anger. 'How could I forget those . . . stockings?' He paused suggestively and the vision of Suzie Lake came between them. Ruth fell silent.

'Altogether an unforgettable day,' he murmured. Then, abruptly, out of the blue, 'Any regrets?'

'Good lord, no!' Caught off guard, she responded vehemently and from the heart, without a second's hesitation, accompanying her words with a fierce little shake of her head which dislodged one of the tortoiseshell combs with which she'd caught back her fast-growing hair. 'Absolutely not!'

He was quicker than she was, as he found the comb in the dewy grass and straightened up to his full height, so that she had to tilt back her head, while he made a clumsy attempt to fix it in place. Beneath his fingers, the baby-fine softness of her hair surprised him.

'Stupid hair,' Ruth muttered quickly. 'These combs just slip out all the time. I must get to a hairdresser before it gets halfway down my back.'

'Leave it alone. I prefer long hair—much more feminine.'

His peremptory tone, the assumption that she would do as he wished, irritated Ruth. Stepping back and out of reach, she went back into role, Sister Silke once more, avoiding intimacy. Lifting her bare arms in an unconsciously graceful gesture, the comb between her small white teeth, she scooped a wing of hair and pinioned it behind her ear with a stabbing motion. Voices called them, and with relief she broke away.

Beneath her high-heeled sandals the lawn was already damp and the air was losing its warmth with the setting sun. She shivered, glad to be joining the others inside. Behind her strolled Dan, ruefully sucking his middle finger. The bloody rose had pricked him. *And* just when he was trying to be gallant and pick a flower for her hair!

In the dining-room overlooking the garden the french windows stood ajar, Charles Raven to her right at the head of the oval mahogany table, the doctor on her left. 'Look at those two,' Dan murmured intimately, his tone mocking, his arm against hers, his lips near her ear. 'She'll be writing his sermons next!'

Ruth stared. Beatrice and Kenneth Richardson? Well, it wasn't her place to comment: but why not? Yes, they certainly seemed very good friends. Aha! Enlightenment dawned. Could it be that Dr Gather was in danger of losing his 'housekeeper' to the vicarage?

Ruth bent her flushed face over her avocado. So the pairings had worked out after all, leaving Ruth Silke to Dan Gather. The doctor and the nurse. How apt. How *very* neat. Was someone doing a bit of matchmaking around here?

They needn't bother! thought Ruth, tight-lipped. Finding another man's the last thing on my mind. So if Dan's in danger of losing Bea and he's looking out for a replacement housekeeper, he can darn well stick to Suzie and stop buttering *me* up to hedge his bets. Look at him now, all over Philippa!

Dan had turned to Philippa on his left and the two were deep in discussion over the English National Opera's latest production of *Don Giovanni*. Philippa was promising to get him tickets.

Ruth concentrated on scraping her empty avocado shell, laughing to herself grimly, for hadn't Dan all the obvious qualifications for the part of the virile Don Giovanni? He might even have a decent baritone, since Danny must have inherited his vocal talent from somewhere.

Charles now engaged her in conversation, and as the evening progressed Ruth regained her normal composure and was able to relax and enjoy the company of her new friends. Charles was taking this informal opportunity to quiz her about herself. He asked about her parents, and over the fresh salmon Ruth explained that her father had died of a heart attack when she was eleven and that her mother was teaching in Devon. That she had a little place of her own in Birmingham, but a nurse friend was going to buy it and the sale was likely to be completed in the next month. Ruth also told him about her sister's small garden centre in Kent which specialised in pinks and pansies.

Everyone, it seemed, loved pinks and pansies. Apart from Dr Gather, who Ruth suspected knew more about the potency of red roses than the shy appeal of a velvety pansy. Anyway, he was entirely ignoring her now he had the far more interesting Philippa for company.

Afterwards, with her husband accompanying her at the grand piano in the drawing-room, Philippa sang *Che faro*? from Gluck's *Orfeo*. It was so beautiful that Ruth was on the verge of tears—'What is life to me without thee?' —and at the end of the evening, when Dan said he would walk her back to the medical centre and as a reward for bravery she could make him some black coffee, Ruth sensibly, and a trifle huffily, observed that the grounds were well lit and she had not the smallest qualm about seeing herself home. And, she thought, gently mocking herself for caring, Dan didn't deserve any kind of reward, the way he'd ignored her for the last half of the evening! 'There's a night nurse sleeping in,' she pointed out. 'I don't need an escort. And none of my patients requires your attention.'

'I don't plan to disturb your patients——'

You're disturbing *me*! thought Ruth. But she bit her lip, and kept silent. Inside her head a protesting voice wailed in frustration: I've had a *very* stressful evening and I'm tired and I want to go to bed.

He dropped his voice and added in low and dramatic tones, 'I'm in need of nursing care myself.'

Her startled face made his eyes glitter. She was lovely to tease. 'I have a thorn in my finger,' he breathed into her ear, making it sound a rare and heart-rending injury. 'I can feel it, hot and throbbing.'

'Shouldn't you take your sister home?' chided Ruth in a don't-be-tiresome-doctor voice. 'It's twenty to twelve.'

'Ken's offered to drop her off.' Dr Gather was either deeply insensitive, or not about to take no for an answer. Either, in Ruth's view, applied in equal measure.

They walked back in silence with at least three feet between them.

Ruth had no intention of taking him into the treatment-room and possibly disturbing the duty nurse.

She made a great show of soundlessly unlocking doors and tiptoeing across the entrance hall, so that he could not fail to get the message that he was causing hassle. She led the way into her sitting-room and motioned Dan to take an easy chair, turning on her heel without waiting to see if he would do so. In the kitchen she kicked off her high heels and filled the electric kettle: instant coffee it would be, and instant bed immediately after. Oh, and of course—that finger.

She yawned loudly and artificially near the open doorway, hoping Dan would take the hint that she wished to be Alone. Carrying a tray, she went back to the sitting-room, only to find he'd disappeared. On the arm of the chair was a novel with his sister's photograph looking out from the dust-cover. Her mother had lent it to her some while ago, promising a darn good read; and Ruth had glanced at *A Bitter Truth* with mild and impersonal interest, but never found time. It struck her now that to return the book personally signed by the author would give Mum no end of a thrill.

She found Dan in her bedroom, standing by her bed, Jeff's picture in his hand. He'd seen it before when she first moved in. 'Your father,' he said.

It took Ruth a second or two to get over the shock of his mistake. Dan must after all have been listening to her conversation with the headmaster.

'My husband,' she said stiffly.

Surprise was evident in the way the doctor looked her up and down, quite obviously surveying her physically and wondering why a nurse in her twenties should elect to marry a man who looked to be thirty years older. Ruth resented this. You didn't choose who to fall in love with!

The age difference had upset her mother too, at first. Jeff had thick, curly grey hair, and a beard half concealing his shrewd weatherbeaten features. He would have been fifty-one next birthday. Normally in excellent health, he had been admitted for surgery—a hernia—timed to fit in with his work as engineering officer for a tanker fleet. That was how they had met.

It was his second marriage—her first. She'd been crazy about him, and had changed her job to work nights, and saved her holidays for the times he was home after long weeks at sea. It hadn't been ideal, the long partings. But oh, when he was home!

Ruth choked back the lump in her throat and said brightly, 'Coffee's ready. I'll take a look at that finger before you go.'

But Dan didn't move. 'Tell me what happened,' he said, and his voice was cool and unemotional. He knew this man was dead, but didn't attempt any sort of gratuitous sympathy.

Ruth kept her composure. Thinking back, later, she realised it hadn't been as hard to speak about it as she would have expected. 'Jeff was a patient—oh, nothing serious. But he was a seaman and had to time his op to coincide with shore leave. His first marriage had ended long before he met me. There were no children. I was in my first sister's post at the QE in Birmingham. We fell in love. It was like a—like a flash fire.' Dan was staring at her so intently, with something in his eyes that seemed to suggest that the cool composed Sister Silke could not be capable of such emotion. Ruth swallowed, determined to finish so that it need never be mentioned again. Dan could tell whomsoever he liked and save her having the bother.

'We were married for just under two years. Jeff moved into my home in Bournville. He was so often away that I took a night sister's post in a private hospital, saving my off-duty for when he was on leave.'

'No children?'

'Jeff didn't want any. We were sufficient for each other.'

Dan was standing with legs apart and folded arms, one speculative finger probing his bottom lip in a gesture that she was beginning to recognise as familiar. There was a certain tension in him, and it transmitted itself to Ruth, who was beginning to feel she could not go on with this, not in her bedroom of all places.

She turned and walked back to the sitting-room and poured Dan's coffee. He had ripped his bow-tie undone and loosened his collar, and black hairs showed at the base of his throat. 'What happened?' he said, cruelly urging her to finish her miserable tale.

Her hands were shaking now and the cup rattled as she handed it to him, hot black liquid slopping into the saucer. 'Jeff was lost at sea. I thought it was a mistake and he would come back. I was always an optimist, you see. My work kept my head above water—hah!' She threw back her head with a bleak laugh at the inappropriate cliché. It came tumbling out now, a torrent of words. 'My father died, you know, in a swimming-pool. In the public baths, of all places. He was teaching me to swim. As a result I'm not very much at home in the water. I never did learn to swim.

'Would you like to read about it?' From a shelf she grabbed a small book of Press cuttings. 'They both made news. Jeff's was headline stuff—you may remember it. Look, see what the *Telegraph* said. And here's *The Times*: "British-owned tanker lost in Iceland storms. Two dead, six reported missing" And look at the date. Christmas.'

With troubled eyes Dan looked down at the child's scrapbook shoved into his hands. He did know how she felt; he'd been there too. Only for him there had been no blind hope to cling to. "The victims included two Britons who were officers of the 10,000-ton tanker which ran aground off the east coast of Iceland at about midnight on Christmas night. Heavy breakers were rolling over the ship . . . an attempt to rescue survivors was hampered by force seven winds, heavy surf and snow showers." God, the poor devils . . . it was madness for her to have dreamed her man could have survived such grim conditions. "The first body was found at 2.40 am, drifting in a life-jacket. Two sank before they could be reached . . ."

Tight-lipped, he closed the book, not wanting to know more. 'Let's have that coffee,' he said quietly. 'Some day I shall tell you my story, but not tonight. We all have our limits, and, poor girl, you're very near yours.' He reached out to put a comforting arm about her shoulders—only to find he'd been talking to himself, Ruth having padded silently away on bare feet.

When Dan came into the sitting-room she took one look at his sombre face and immediately regretted having embarrassed him with her tale of woe. Mustering all her flagging spirits, she put on a pretence of matter-of-fact normality, filling his cup—black coffee, as he'd requested—with a rock-steady hand and chatting about the dinner party with a brittle fervour that fooled neither of them. Dan agreed to get her mother's book signed, and then changed his mind and said, 'Come to supper and ask Bea yourself.'

'That would be lovely,' lied Ruth, who now had a thumping headache and was feeling slightly sick.

'I almost forgot!' she exclaimed loudly, and jumped up for the third time, to fetch her sewing basket and advance upon Dan with a needle.

'Hold on!' he protested. 'I don't want gangrene, thank you very much!'

'Don't be such a fusspot. I'm only having a quick look before I stick it in the gas flame.' She managed a wanly flirtatious smile. 'It's hardly in my interests, Dr Gather, to render you *hors de combat*.'

'Yes,' he agreed drily. 'I'd noticed you were fond of a bit of combat. Ouch! That hurts.'

What nice hands he's got, thought Ruth, squeezing the offending finger. 'Oh, yes, here we are. I'll have that out in a jiffy. Hang on while I sterilise my instruments of torture and set up a blood transfusion,' she joked, adding briskly, 'and it would be a big help if you wouldn't mind standing up so I can get at you.'

He obliged on the instant with an athletic bound that had him towering over Ruth, whose eyes fixed recklessly on the warm V of olive skin revealed by his open-throated evening shirt. A ribbon of Paisley silk hung loose about his neck—none of your ready-tied bows for the suave Dr Dan. She was feeling quite breathless now, the nausea forgotten, replaced by a giddy awareness of the lateness of the hour and the sexual tension produced by close proximity with this hugely attractive man. Her head bent over his hand so that he couldn't see what she was doing, and this was deliberate because for some daft reason her own hand seemed to be composed of a mass of vibrating nerves.

'Will you catch me if I faint, Nurse?' he murmured in voice that was more rich dark sherry than weak tea.

Questioningly Ruth lifted her head and forced her gaze to travel swiftly past that hard sardonic mouth to meet his laughing black eyes. Her lips twitched in response. Teasing was a game two could play. 'I know I'm a big girl, Dr Gather, but if you faint on me, I'll leave you right down there on the carpet . . .

'Look at that!' she exclaimed in satisfaction as her probing released a brute of a thorn. 'You were very brave, and you shall have one of my badges.'

'Oh, no, not the Ruth Silke fan club?' mocked Dan, at which Ruth blushed dreadfully, muttered something about having left the gas on, and dashed into the kitchen to stare in horror at her rosy image in the small mirror over the cooker and the blush that ran from the roots of her hair, down her neck and into her burning décolletage.

'See you Monday,' yawned Dan, sticking his head round the kitchen door. 'Thanks for the TLC.'

And with that he was gone.

The next day was Sunday.

Ruth woke up and realised she had a problem. Her pretty dress lay crumpled on the carpet where she'd dropped it and her pyjamas were still neatly folded beneath her pillow. Something ominous was threatening to disrupt her orderly life.

She had fallen in love with Dr Gather.

Well, she'd just have to fall *out* of love with him, simple as that. *Loving* someone: that was permanent and something one couldn't help. But *'in love'* was an alterable condition, a sort of illness, an infatuation that mind over matter could cure and in her particular case *had* to! Otherwise this wonderful job would turn into a hell on earth. She fell back dreamily on to the pillows. What a night they'd had together! She'd never done things like *that*—and then some!—with any man but Jeff, who'd been an ardent and enthusiastic lover. It was scandalous! She'd gone to bed blushing and woken up positively scarlet with total recall! Thank heaven it was all in her own silly head and no one but she could ever know that she'd dreamed Dan hadn't left the san after all, that they'd spent an indescribably passionate night together . . .

In chapel she turned moist-eyed at the sight of the children's scrubbed and innocent faces, at the way the little ones put their hands together and screwed their eyes tight as they prayed for their mummies and daddies and sisters and brothers and Rover and Fluffy back home, and she wondered how parents could bear to pack their seven-year-olds off to boarding schools: even one as happy as Ditchingham House. Her roaming gaze alighted on Danny, seated in the choir stalls and looking pleased as Punch in his new robes. He hadn't got a wicked stepmother after all! Poor Beatrice deserved a halo rather than a witch's hat . . .

Bea must be longing for the day when Dan remarried; she probably saw Sister Silke as a sensible sort of choice.

Ruth sighed and fixed her eyes on the headmaster,

who was addressing the congregation from the pulpit. Pity Dan had to have his say in the matter, because Ruth would gladly mother his darling children and mind his house and cook his meals. But sadly she'd never match up to Suzie Lake in the glamour girl stakes.

There was a shuffling of feet as the choir alone stood to sing an unaccompanied anthem and the director of music stepped out into the chancel nave to conduct them. His wife, Philippa, wasn't in the congregation, but perhaps she'd had to drive away to her next opera engagement. Ruth wondered how her husband felt about having the school's charismatic doctor pay Philippa such close attention. A ladies' man, if ever there was one. And all that fuss about a thorn he could have dealt with in a couple of seconds himself! Just a ploy to chat Ruth up, too, because Philippa was out of bounds and he was in the mood . . .

There was nothing especially flattering about being one among many, ruminated the school nurse, pulling her thoughts together with a guilty start as she realised the anthem had finished and she hadn't taken in a single note.

That night she was roused from a dreamless sleep by the shrilling of the telephone. It was the housemaster of St Margaret's. 'Sorry to bother you at this hour, Ruth, but could you come across and have a look at Marina O'Brien? I don't want to call Dan out unless you feel it's absolutely necessary.'

Ruth shuddered agreement. She was doing well so far and didn't fancy a relapse in the early days of her cure . . . 'I'll be right over,' she promised comfortingly, and heard the relief in the speaker's voice as he thanked her and set down the phone.

CHAPTER EIGHT

'SISTER!'

'Coming!' called Ruth from the office. She pressed Close Edit and instructed the computer to suspend the document she was working on. It took mere seconds.

In the hall was Mr Evans, and with him a boy with his head tipped back and a blood-soaked handkerchief pressed to his nose.

'Richard got bashed with a cricket ball,' the teacher explained. 'I've put a key down his back, but he's still gushing. Aren't you?'

'Yes, sir,' a muffled voice agreed throatily.

Ruth pinched the top of Richard's nose, with her other hand tugging his bloodstained cricket shirt out of his white flannels. A door key fell to the floor with a clang and Mr Evans picked it up. 'I'd better have this back,' he said. 'It didn't seem to do much good.'

Ruth gave him a dry look. 'I'm afraid that's an old wives' tale,' she said tartly, guiding her patient in the direction of the nearest sink. He was a tall lad, almost as tall as she was, and well built with the promise of powerful shoulders and strong bare arms under rolled-up sleeves. One of those in their last term at Ditchingham House.

'It is OK if I leave him with you? Only I've left my class unsupervised.'

Ruth nodded, her left eyebrow raised. Keys down the back indeed! You would expect a teacher to have more

116

sense.

She turned her attention to reassuring the boy. 'Now don't worry about all the blood. It looks like a lot, but it isn't really. Breathe gently through your mouth. I'm going to feel the shape of the bone . . . yes, that's fine. You can sit up now. I'm going to put an ice pack across the bridge of your nose to try and stop the bleeding.'

Richard sat up, a bit pale, but grinning to himself. 'I knew about the key business,' he confided, 'but I didn't like to tell Mr Evans. My dad's an orthopaedic surgeon.'

'Top marks for tact!' applauded Ruth, sharing the boy's amusement.

The phone rang in the office, but she was holding the compress in place, so she left it. Mrs Downie would take the call on the ward extension. Sure enough, a few moments later her footsteps could be heard in the corridor.

'That was Dr Gather, enquiring about the child with the eczema flare-up. I told him she was much more comfortable today. He wants you to ring him back before evening surgery.'

'Will do.'

Mrs Downie came into the room and looked at Richard. 'And what have you been up to?'

'Got in the way of a cricket ball——'

'But nothing broken, I'm happy to say. Let's see how we're doing, Richard . . . there, it's slowing up already.'

'That shirt ought to go into some cold water,' advised Mrs Downie. 'I'll see to it if you can slip it off. There's some T-shirts in the linen cupboard, you can borrow one of those.'

On the way out, Richard was thrilled to see one of his

paintings on display by the front door. 'I wondered what
Mr Jolly had done with my Tolkien. He never told me
it was on the wall! Look—there's my initials, R.H., for
Richard Harrison.'

'That's one of my favourites! You haven't given it a
title, but I knew it was *The Lord of the Rings*. And
you've used colour so dramatically. I'll make sure you
get this back for end of term.'

End of term was only a few weeks away. How the
time had flown!

'Keep the picture if you'd like to, Sister Silke.'

Ruth was sincerely touched. 'Are you *sure*? Hey,
keep that head still . . . How very kind of you! Promise
you'll bring your parents over here to see it.'

'And Richard,' she called after him, 'don't blow your
nose today if you can possibly help it. Otherwise we
might have to resort to nasal packs!'

Richard pulled a face, waved, and went back to the
cricket field to watch the rest of the game.

Ruth rang Dan.

Perhaps he had remembered his vague invitation to
supper, made several weeks ago after that unsettling
disagreement over Danny. She understood now what he
meant about his sister Bea and her cooking and being
'on another planet'. Of course Bea couldn't have
interrupted a flourishing career to look after her much
younger and recently widowed brother's children. Shut
away in her study she was indeed in a world of her own
creating, which accounted for the bewildered voice that
had answered the telephone when Ruth had rung to
explain about Danny's accident. And cooking and
shopping and planning meals, all that was

understandably an unwelcome interruption to a writer's day. She could offer to take along a pudding, perhaps a trifle or Jeff's favourite raspberry Pavlova. There'd be raspberries in the shops by now.

Already Ruth was thinking about what to wear and what sort of house Dan lived in—it would be old and rambling and have bags of character, maybe a ghost; and she could ask Bea to sign a book for her mother.

'Yes?' snapped a peremptory voice.

Ruth the woman disappeared and Sister Silke RGN took her place. 'Dr Gather?' She knew it was he, but what a way to answer a telephone!

'Speaking. Is that you, Ruth?' He always called her Ruth now. And rarely did she respond as informally. The secrets of her heart were not for sharing. Work served as a safety barrier between them.

'You wanted me to call you back.'

'Mmm.' He seemed to have forgotten why. Or else his mind was on more important things.

'Is there a problem?' she asked curtly, for she was still on duty and not given to making personal calls in school time.

'Did I tell you I shall be away for the next three days?'

'You did not.' And what am I supposed to do if I need you?

'I'm going to a conference in Brighton—child health surveillance in the nineties. I'll be back on Wednesday night.'

'Oh.' Ruth felt her shoulder sag, her spirits deflate. 'What do I do if I need you?' she asked, unaware that she sounded so despondent.

Dan grinned, but kept his reply brusque. 'Need me?

You seem to manage pretty well without me. Call Philip, my partner.'

Ruth tucked a loose strand of hair behind her ear, and said sorry, of course, she'd forgotten about Dr Bishop, and have a good time.

'See you Thursday,' he said, and rang off.

The phone shrilled as soon as she put the receiver down. It was the head of Pre-prep. 'I've a poor little person here with a nasty grazed knee and elbow and in deep distress. Shall I get someone with a car to pop her over to you?'

'Oh, dear!' commiserated Ruth. 'No, don't trouble, I'll come across. I shan't be long.'

Assembling a portable medical kit, she hurried out of the building, first telling Mrs Downie where she was going.

The sunshine was dazzling. Ruth told herself she couldn't remember a summer like it—mellow heat by day and showery in the deepest hours of the night, so that the cricket pitches were as perfect as on the cover of the school prospectus, the buildings set among emerald lawns and elegant treescapes in every conceivable shade of green. Late June had filled the rose-beds with colour and the giant wisteria sprawling over the main building, now past its flowery prime, was shedding a carpet of papery rust and mauve petals, which crunched beneath Ruth's brown lace-up shoes as she strode along.

From the swimming-pool came splashings and the sound of children's happy voices. The tennis-courts were in full swing and a batsman was taking guard on the neatly mown cricket strip, with the fielding team very properly dressed in white, as one of the younger masters supervised the game. In summer, cricket was serious business indeed at Ditchingham House.

The patient was Rosie Gather's best friend, Olivia May. While the rest of the class were having story-time, Ruth was taken to the staff room where she cleansed and anointed and dressed the sore little knee and elbow —Rosie hovering by, big brown eyes agog, passing Ruth her scissors and being most helpful.

It was an elementary piece of first aid that anyone could have undertaken, but Miss Decker was quite embarrassingly grateful. Rosie led her friend back to the classroom, carefully holding her hand and glancing back across her shoulder to smile shyly at her Daddy's nurse from the san.

Ruth saw an attractive woman with short dark hair beginning to turn grey, smooth pink and white skin and a tender disposition that found Olivia's pain distressing. Now in her mid-forties, Josephine Decker had never married and the school, Ruth could tell, was the most important thing in her life. Perhaps this will be me in twenty years' time, wondered Ruth to herself . . .

Miss Decker insisted on apologising for troubling Ruth. 'Generally we can deal with minor accidents ourselves, but Olivia screamed the place down and wouldn't let any of my staff help her. You've got the magic touch, Sister, and no mistake!'

Ruth smiled and shook her head, observing sympathetically that it must have been quite a nasty tumble. 'Rosie was very concerned, wasn't she?'

'Our Rosie is always first on the spot to "gather" the fallen! A born nurse, yes, indeed. You should just see the little drawings she does of herself in a nurse's uniform with a big red cross on the front and white caps, just like Matron wore.'

Ruth had to smile. 'Not a doctor?'

'Oh, definitely not. And she's cute enough to know the difference. She's the kindest little girl. It's quite unusual for a four-year-old to show such concern for others. Children are generally very self-centred at that age.'

Ruth collected her things together and was just about to make her way back when it occurred to her that Miss Decker might be able to cast new light on the problem of Rosie's brother.

'Danny has worried me rather—he has so many accidents. Would you say he's a happy child?'

'Danny's only been in the main school since September. He was with me for the best part of three years, so I know him pretty well and basically I would say he's a well-adjusted boy. I'll tell you what I think. He's old enough to know that his mother died soon after Rosie was born, and young enough to be afraid deep down that the same thing might happen to his father.'

Yes, Ruth had suspected that was part of it. 'But would you describe him as accident prone?'

A bell rang, classroom doors opened, and children began to file out to get their coats, the teachers supervising them and insisting on a quiet and orderly end to the school day.

'Come into my study,' invited Miss Decker. 'If I shut the door, then it means I'm not to be disturbed. I need to think about this.'

The two women settled opposite each other in

battered easy chairs, a shaft of afternoon sun surrounding the teacher's earnest head in a halo of gold. Ruth was grateful for the chance to discuss Danny Gather with someone who knew him well, but who could make an objective assessment of his state of mind.

Finally Miss Decker concluded that she had to agree with Dr Gather.

Danny was not, in her estimation, a troubled child, unconsciously causing himself injury to gain his father's attention. He was, though, highly intelligent, imaginative, and physically bold. Just the sort of boy who'd have a go at anything which appealed to his sense of adventure. 'Does that help?' she asked.

'It does indeed,' said Ruth. 'I confess I've been worrying about that child ever since I came to the school. I ventured to share this with Dr Gather, but got short shrift from him. I'm afraid he must have felt I was being critical of the way he brings up his children, when nothing was further from my mind.'

'He's a good man. It was desperately sad when his wife died, and I think we all hoped it wouldn't be too long before he remarried, for his own and the children's sake.' Miss Decker patted her hair rather selfconsciously and Ruth couldn't help noticing that her cheeks were growing pinker than ever. 'But . . . time goes by.'

Ruth had been wondering whom she could ask. Obviously not Dan himself. Nor Gwyneth Raven, who might suspect a fluttering heart where the personable, and very eligible, school doctor was concerned. Particularly if the school nurse started making enquiries about her dishy colleague's personal circumstances.

But how exactly had Mrs Gather died?

Jo Decker was sure to know, patiently tending her own fluttering heart, poor woman . . .

And how many others were mooning over Dr Dan? Any female with red blood in her veins! warned a knowing little voice inside Ruth's sensible head. No wonder he was so damn sure of himself.

But her curiosity was going to have to remain unsatisfied for a while longer. Already the school clock was striking three-thirty, its boom sounding louder than Ruth was used to. Pre-prep was silent, only the four teachers and the nurse still in the building. Carol Downie would be late getting away if Ruth didn't get a move on.

Time seemed to drag with Dan in Brighton. The hours were endless.

Far from having problems, all was quiet in the medical centre, the ward empty, the children blossoming in the sunshine. So the headmaster suggested Ruth take a day off. Ruth drove into Bath and treated herself to lunch, shopping, and sightseeing. But lovely as the city was, she found herself hurrying back to the car park with a smile on her face and her arms full of packages, eager to get back 'home'. She had bought shoes *and* the sandals she was wearing, from Russell & Bromley—expensive, but an excellent fit for her long narrow feet; a French Connection pink denim sun-dress, very bare and strappy; two T-shirts and a pair of white shorts from Benetton *and* their flowery trousers, which she would have thought she could not possibly get away with, but which, once tried on, were so pretty and flattering that the shop assistant wouldn't take no for an answer! And some delicious underwear from a small specialist shop, tucked away in a back street, which she had discovered quite by accident. She had peered wide-eyed at the window display and been drawn inside, where she found herself in a sultan's harem of lace-dripping silks and satins that were quite irresistible, and about as sensible as giving cream cakes to cardiac patients. In other words, pretty likely to cause abnormal heart rhythms.

You're off your trolley! criticised that voice in her head with which she seemed to be having so many arguments lately. Pure silk! You'll have to wash that lot by hand. And who's to see you in it, may I ask?

Ruth just shrugged and smiled, not in the least caring if no one ever did. Sometimes it could be quite exhilarating to step out of character and do something outrageous - like pay some attention to what one put on one's back, for instance!

She wasn't a girl to turn heads in the streets. And no one stared as her long legs took her round the streets of Bath. No make-up, her fair hair fluffy from the morning's shampoo, in a simple white blouse and loose beige trousers rolled up above bare ankles, smart brown sandals on her slim bare feet.

The next afternoon, she and Carol took wooden chairs and sat outside the entrance, sipping iced lemonade and stretching out pale bare legs to catch the sun, feeling thankful that no child was unwell and at the same time guilty because they were not needed. There was not much to look at: the small parking area and its laurel hedge, with playing-fields over to the right glimpsed through the silver birches. But anything was better than being inside on a day like this.

'Doctor'll be all right in Brighton,' observed Mrs Downie, nodding up at the cobalt sky. 'Just the place I'd like to be. I'd give my back teeth for a swim, wouldn't you, Sister? Wonder if he'll go sunbathing on *that* beach —you know the one I mean.'

It wasn't usual for Mrs Downie to come up with remarks like that, and Ruth felt it wiser not to encourage idle chat about Dr Gather.

'I'm sure they'll have their noses to the grindstone, Mrs Downie,' she said in a no-nonsense tone. Then, immediately sorry she had pulled rank, she offered to fetch more of her home-made lemonade.

When she came back, Mrs Downie said what lovely sandals, and Ruth said she had bought them in Bath, finding her lace-up shoes too warm in this weather. Mrs Downie always wore Scholls, winter and summer.

They sipped their drinks.

'Only fifteen more days . . .' murmured Ruth, speaking her thoughts aloud. Whatever was she going to do with herself for nearly two whole months?

Her mother's term went on to the end of July and then she was going to La Manga for three weeks with friends from her golf club. Ruth supposed she could go and give her sister a hand at the garden centre. The Birmingham house was now sold. She had nothing special planned and she hated to be idle. She wondered if her contract would allow her to do agency nursing in one of the Birmingham hospitals.

'Jim and I brought our lads up here last summer holidays,' Mrs Downie was saying, 'with Mr Raven's permission, of course. Dr Gather used to come down too, with little Rosie and young Danny. The children played together so nicely, and Rosie learned to swim ever so quickly.'

That didn't do much to boost Ruth's confidence, hearing that Dan's four-year-old could do something she found terrifying.

'If you're here in August, you'll get some lovely swims.'

'I—I can't,' Ruth confessed.

'You'll be going away, Sister? Abroad, somewhere nice?'

Ruth shrugged. 'I haven't made any plans. Actually, I meant, I can't swim. I never learned.' She smoothed her skirt and then said with a brittle laugh, 'I seem to have a thing about water. It dates back to childhood.'

Mrs Downie was most sympathetic. She patted Ruth's shoulder and said her elder sister fell into a canal at the age of three and for *years* wouldn't do more than paddle at the seaside. But she'd been to a special adult class and now she could even dive. 'You should get Dr Gather to teach you, some quiet evening. He's ever so good and patient. Not like my Jim. When I was learning to drive, I tell you, I could happily have murdered . . .'

Dr Gather . . . good and patient . . . Get Dr Gather to teach you . . .

Carol chatted on, blissfully ignorant of the trauma this suggestion had produced in the calm and capable sister-in-charge.

Ruth sat with arms folded, her fingers digging into her flesh, her neck stiff with tension, not knowing whether to laugh or cry at the discovery that somewhere in her sensible grey matter lurked a startlingly vivid imagination.

Dan in skimpy black swimming-trunks and looking overpoweringly, *threateningly* gorgeous as he made a grab for her. Herself a huge white whale bursting out of a bikini designed for a water sprite . . . Heaven help me! agonised Ruth, the flow of Carol's chat going in one ear and out the other. The irony of Carol's suggestion! Far from keeping her head above water, the treatment Dan Gather preferred for a troublesome woman—and wouldn't she just fit that diagnosis to a T!—was to submerge her good and thoroughly.

The sight of a racily driven red sports car, careering in from the drive and juddering to a halt beside Ruth's dusty Metro, jolted her back to something approaching normality. The hood was down, and the driver, female, wore Rayban sun-specs and a pink chiffon headscarf tied Grace Kelly style.

Carol, anyway, wasn't batting an eyelid. 'It's Miss Gather,' she observed comfortably. 'Shall I bring her some of your home-made lemonade, Sister?'

'Please do, there's a jug in my fridge.'

Ruth turned with outstretched hand to greet Bea Gather, now struggling out of the low bucket seat and unveiling her neat grey perm. You'd have expected her to have come straight from the WI rather than a red-hot word processor.

Her opening, as Ruth was later ruefully to reflect, was deceptively simple:

'I'm picking up Rosie today. And since for once—*mirabile dictu*!—I'm actually early, I thought I should drop by and see how you're getting on . . .'

When Dan walked in, he looked as if he'd spent the whole darn conference on a Brighton beach. He'd discarded his jacket and was wearing a white shirt with the sleeves rolled up, just to make sure everybody noticed what a good tan he'd picked up.

Ruth had been waiting for him, clock-watching with an eagerness that hardly matched the occasion. After all, Dan was the visiting medical officer, and, Ruth had managed to kid herself—unaware of her eyelids growing heavy at the sight of him, and her pupils dilating into telltale black spheres—physical attraction had nothing to do with it.

'Hello there!' he said, eyeing her up and down as if to remind himself of her body image. 'You're looking well. Got freckles on your nose, Sister.'

'And half a dozen pounds on my rear end,' muttered Ruth to herself behind a bland smile. She hated him examining her like that. It was hardly polite.

'You're looking very fit, Doctor,' she responded primly. Maybe if they emptied the swimming-pool first! Quickly she had to smother the naughty giggle that threatened to surface.

'Very brown,' she went on, allowing herself to glance briefly up at him from under her lashes. 'I *do* hope they didn't work you too hard.' Stop flirting! scolded her conscience. What's the matter with you today? You know he's not to be trusted. Don't give him any encouragement. Remember Philippa. Remember Suzie Lake.

'I wasn't lazing about on *that* beach, Sister Silke. And I got tanned walking along the front for an hour each afternoon, so it's as you see, only from the neck up.'

Ruth put on a patient expression that she hoped would irritate Dan into further indiscretions. What a funny mood she was in today. Not at all her normal self, she felt sort of reckless. Because it was lovely to have him back.

'When you've finished reminiscing,' she sighed teasingly, leaning over to switch on the computer, one bare leg and sandalled foot outstretched to balance her body, 'we'll get on with some proper work. We've forty minutes before the children I want you to see come across from the main school—and you'll be glad to know I've an empty ward for you today.'

She settled down in front of the keyboard, very aware of Dan close beside her, swivelling the VDU so they both could see the screen. She programmed the machine, loaded the disc drive and began working through her list of requests for prescription renewals. Dan scribbled away on his prescription pad—for a doctor his writing was reasonable—and on screen Ruth amended the drugs records. From time to time he would take hold of her right wrist to stop her typing and Ruth would scarcely breathe as his fingers hovered over her pulse. Supposedly he was satisfying himself there were no inadvertent errors.

'I can spell, you know.'

'Yes, yes, just making sure. And the next?'

'Ventolin, please, for Emily Porter and James Morton-Hunt.'

'When was the last prescription? This year?'

When they'd finished, she went to make the coffee, as usual, bringing the tray to the office and calling Mrs

Downie to join them.

Dan took the one easy chair as of right, his long legs in immaculately creased grey flannels stretched out so that the nurses would have to step over him. 'Used to take ages when I did that with Matron. Everything written down longhand.'

'Yes, a computer's a marvellous help.'

'So, you've had a quiet week. You deserve it.'

'Thanks,' acknowledged Sister Silke, handing the doctor the black coffee he'd asked for.

'Danny been behaving himself?'

'He generally does, to the best of my knowledge,' came Ruth's cool response. In spite of the arrangement made between herself and Bea Gather—and which Dan was not yet aware of—she still preferred to dissociate herself from the implication of any special involvement with the doctor's son.

'Course he has, Doctor!' said Mrs Downie, who was bothered by no such inhibitions. 'He's a grand little lad, your Danny. The image of you, if you don't mind me saying so. And his sister's a cutie-pie. They're the nicest kiddies and have lovely manners. I know you must be very proud of your two.'

Dan unclasped his hands from behind his neck and launched himself out of the chair, acknowledging as he did so, and rather brusquely Ruth felt, 'You're very kind to say so, Mrs Downie. And now, Sister, I think I hear the patter of muddy feet . . .'

In walked a tracksuited Angus Stewart, frowning down at his white trainers as he picked up the doctor's remark. He nodded at Carol and raised his eyebrows at Ruth, a gesture which Dan misinterpreted and which cooled the atmosphere by several frosty degrees.

Carol collected the coffee-tray and made herself scarce.

The two big handsome men faced each other. 'I don't know whether Ruth's said anything to you——' Angus began.

Ruth shook her head. Hell! She'd forgotten.

CHAPTER NINE

ANGUS stripped off his tracksuit top, grimacing as he pulled his arms free. 'Could you take a look at my elbow, Dan?' he asked with the familiarity of his generation. For he was a good ten years younger. And it showed in his lack of style, noted Ruth, waiting nervously for the doctor to suggest Mr Stewart make an appointment for evening surgery.

Dan was abrupt, even unfriendly. Yet Angus was a perfectly nice young man—good-looking, easygoing; if not very interesting, in Ruth's estimation.

'Tennis elbow,' grunted Dan after a cursory glance at the red and swollen elbow Angus was holding up for inspection. 'Had any trouble before?'

'Nope. Ruth suggested I try twisting a towel in opposite directions.'

'Did she, indeed?' said Dan with deep uninterest. He looked across at Ruth with a black glare that said 'Didn't I tell you to steer clear of this guy?' 'Jailer's elbow, pudding mixer's elbow, golfer's elbow, Cresta Runner's elbow—all the same condition. You're a sportsman, you ought to know about sports injuries.'

'Well, I—er——'

Ruth bit her lip and moved closer to poor Angus, who was no match for Dan in verbal games. She put her cool fingers on his arm. The skin over the inflammation was burning hot. Angus had told her it was hellishly painful.

Her blue eyes were tinged with violet as they gazed

reproachfully at the doctor.

Angus, however, had found his tongue and was remembering what he'd learned at PE college. 'A condition caused by excessive backward stretching of tendons attached to the fingers.'

'Dorsiflexion,' murmured Dan, with a smile that was somehow far from encouraging.

Ruth was outraged. He had no right to treat Angus like a schoolboy!

But Angus wasn't so easily crushed. 'And it *will* heal by itself . . . eventually,' he came back sarcastically. 'Only in my job I can't afford to wait that long. I'm instructing in a summer camp after term ends. So, Doc, have you anything in your black bag that might help?'

'Sit down,' said Dan in a more kindly fashion. 'Now I wouldn't want to recommend cortisone injections unless you were having severe problems. What I'd suggest you try now is a pack of frozen peas—wrapped in cloth and held over your elbow to reduce the inflammation. And rest the joint in a simple arm sling—Ruth can see to that for you. I'm going to prescribe you an anti-inflammatory which can be picked up from the chemist along with the rest of the school's prescriptions——'

Children's voices could be heard in the entrance hall. Ruth went to the door and said, 'Wait in line till I call you. And wait quietly.'

'Yes, Sister Silke,' intoned the voices, followed by a shuffling of feet and whispers.

Back inside the office Dan was saying, 'And I've personally found that buying a tennis racket with a thicker handle than the one you usually use reduces pressure on the muscles of the forearm and solves the problem.'

A fellow sufferer! Ruth heaved a private sigh of relief. She hadn't for one moment believed Dan would allow personal dislike to take precedence over professional concern; and she'd been proved right. As she waited to shepherd her patients in to see the doctor, Angus emerged fully dressed, giving her a broad wink which made the children giggle.

'I'll come back later and you can strap me up,' he said loudly as he left. This made Ruth titter and Dr Dan mutter under his breath.

At the end of the session, Ruth said, her head tilted to one side so that her cap sat at an angle of forty-five degrees, 'I don't understand what it is about Angus that seems to annoy you.'

'The way he hangs around you,' said Dan baldly.

It was ridiculous, but he sounded just like a jealous lover. Ridiculous, but intriguing . . .

Acting puzzled, Ruth protested, 'But it's our free time. Angus isn't taking me away from the children.' The truth was that she didn't see much of Angus at all; once he had tried her out and found her chilly as a fridge, there had been no more invitations to steamy films or hot suppers. But they remained on amicable terms, and Ruth was the first person to whom Angus had brought his elbow.

There was a long silence, which Ruth finally broke. 'Dr Gather, if you're in any way dissatisfied with my work, please say so. If there's something I should have been——'

His frown and the abrupt flick of his hand interrupted

her. 'No, of course there isn't! You should know by now,
I'm very direct. If I've got criticisms, I make them to
the person concerned. I hate a lot of muttering behind
people's backs.'

This gave Ruth her chance. She didn't say 'Liar!' But
she came close to reminding Dan of his terse warnings
that her 'angel' of a helper might have very unangelic
intentions towards her—and was noted for skills other
than carpentry. She wasn't going to let Dan know it, but
yes, she'd pretty soon realised Angus liked to play the
field and was popular among the younger staff, who
included several single women. And Angus himself was
such a wholesome, handsome, *uncomplicated* hunk. He
had not been in the least unpleasant towards Ruth,
remaining just as friendly, but transferring his lust to the
tiny blonde who had recently joined them as the bursar's
secretary.

Triumphant in her logic, she pointed out to Dan that
he had hardly given Angus Stewart the benefit of his
'advice', had he? And here Ruth made the grave mistake
of letting Dan know she knew what she knew. 'But
then,' she added provocatively, 'you're hardly qualified
to advise others on the conduct of their private affairs,
are you, Doctor?'

Dan looked astonished. His right eyebrow nearly hit
his hairline. He would be wondering who could have
told her. But then he had no idea she had remained
friendly with Suzie, and he must have forgotten she had
seen him giving Philippa the Treatment.

His astonishment was supplanted by a cold black
anger that made Ruth back away, her throat suddenly
dry. Automatically, her two hands flew to her mouth as

if to seal it against further indiscretion. She wished she hadn't said that—oh, how she wished she hadn't said it! But it was too late now. And Dan was going to go home and most likely have Bea tell him of her marvellous 'arrangement'.

She just had to apologise before he left.

'I am sorry,' she said, and her voice ached with sincerity. Her eyes clung to his, appeal in their sky-blue depths. 'I shouldn't have said that—I'd no right. It was just that you seemed to have such a down on Angus and I was concerned to know why.'

Dan was regarding her with such utter disdain that Ruth could hardly bear it. Her apology got swept aside.

'I failed to appreciate,' he said with biting sarcasm, 'that you were such a Doris Day that you'd need it spelling out in capital letters. Have fun kissing him better, won't you? Plenty of TLC and he'll soon have two good arms to grope you with.'

Ruth's jaw dropped at the sheer blatant cheek of the man. Words failed her. She stood rooted to the spot, fists clenched, her head reeling as if it had been subjected to a knock-out blow.

Dan stalked out without saying goodbye, his leg brushing the skirt of her dress when she didn't move aside.

'Doris Day?' she muttered aloud. For heaven's sake, *why Doris Day*?

Ruth was in the habit of listening to the radio as she cleaned her rooms. For housework she wore jeans and her old check shirt, and fixed her growing hair in a ponytail she considered much too *infra dig* for her years, but she would smarten herself up after the cleaning was done. She started with the bathroom, washing the floor and polishing the chrome taps till they shone, then moved on to the bedroom, going into every nook and cranny with the Hoover and doing the same to the sitting-room. She listened to the Daily Service, and sang along with the hymns which she was getting to know and enjoy from the services in chapel. And then came *Down Your Way* and a short programme on poetry requests, some of which were lovely and very moving, especially one about a dead hedgehog, by Philip Larkin, which said we should all be kind to one another while there was still time. It brought tears to Ruth's eyes and she resolved to try to be very kind to Dr Gather whom, sometimes, she very much disliked.

She was on her knees in the sitting-room when the smooth-voiced announcer said: 'And now for a programme about a star of the fifties and sixties cinema, who is coming back into fashion as society turns away from permissiveness and back to old-style morality—Doris Day.'

Ruth's ears pricked up on the instant.

She sat up on her haunches, leaning over to turn up the sound on her transistor radio. Of course, she had heard of Doris Day; but she couldn't remember any of her films. Doris of the apple cheeks and broad grin and very blonde short hair.

Ruth could see no physical resemblance between herself and the star. It must be the goody-goody image Dan was comparing her with. Ruth felt very hurt. But she was curious to listen and find out more. And naught for your comfort! warned a voice inside her head.

All the same, a duster clutched in her lap, she sat back
and listened.

The strong confident voice filled the room. What a
great singer! The words of the song struck a chord in
Ruth, too. She jumped to her feet and clapped her hands
in agreement, galvanised into action. Switch the radio
off, and waste no more time. I've heard quite enough.
It that's Doris Day, then she's got her head screwed on
the right way and I'm a fan.

'Blonde, wholesome, appealing,' said the film critic,
'but low on *sex* appeal, Doris's old-maidishness——'

Ruth snapped off the radio. So that was what he'd
meant!

The kitchen took the brunt of her indignant energy.
If Dan Gather walked through that door right this
minute he'd get more than a lashing from this old maid's
tongue! He'd get a bucket of soapy water right over his
arrogant chauvinist head! Low in sex appeal, was she?
Huh! Being kind to hedgehogs was the *last* thing on
Ruth's mind.

With the children looking forward to home and summer
holidays, the last two days of term would be uneventful.
Or so Ruth was hoping. That would mean she had no
need to face Dr Gather again—at least, before the
August Arrangement.

Term ended on the Wednesday. On Tuesday, after the
two o'clock break, one of the Pre-prep day children put
the fear of God into her teacher by tearfully saying she
had eaten some berries and her tummy hurt.

The child was bundled into a car and rushed round to
Ruth with commendable urgency.

Lindy was crying and confused; too confused by all the attention she was getting to tell them anything at all about the berries or where she'd found them. Jo Decker was very calm, but white as a sheet.

Ruth examined the little girl very carefully, taking note of the pupil size and checking inside her mouth, as she took her pulse and asked if she felt sick. Lindy shook her head.

'Can you tell me, sweetheart, where you found the berries?' she encouraged.

'I don't remember,' wept Lindy, terrified by all these adults bending over her, and all these questions and frowning faces. She buried her face in Ruth's shoulder and refused to stop crying. 'My tummy hurts,' she wailed, 'I want my mummy!'

'Did you eat them at break, Lindy? You must tell us, dear, then we can make your tummy better.'

Miss Decker wrung her hands and shook her head. 'I can't think how she could have got hold of any poisonous berries. We don't let them out of our sight, and their play area is right by the school building, as you know, with the swings and the climbing-frame and the logs.'

It didn't seem possible, but she asked all the same, squatting down to put herself on a level with Lindy, who was sitting on Ruth's lap and clinging to the nurse as if her life depended on it. 'You haven't been down near the vegetable garden, have you, Lindy? No?' Jo Decker raised a worried face to Ruth and whispered fearfully, 'Are you going to have to use a stomach-pump?'

'Oh no,' whispered back Ruth with a faint smile and a comforting shake of her head. 'I'll give her a dose of ipecacuanha in lots of orange juice and get her to be sick in a bucket. Then we can see what it is she's eaten and take it from there. I don't think it's anything too awful. She's a good colour and not in shock; not apparently very ill apart from a sore stomach. She isn't hyperventilating and her pulse is fine—a bit fast, but then she's frightened.'

Lindy began to calm down and her sobs became hiccups which gradually turned into snuffles of self-pity. Ruth's frilly cap seemed to fascinate her, so Ruth took it off and popped it on the child's head. 'Mummy said they weren't ripe and we'd be sick,' Lindy suddenly volunteered, right out of the blue.

Ruth and Jo Decker exchanged surprised glances. 'What wasn't ripe, Lindy?' Ruth promptly very gently.

'The green things what my bruvver picked. With the prickles on. I scratched myself—look.' Sure enough, the backs of the plump little hands were faintly scratched from the thorny bushes.

Miss Decker thumped herself on the chest in relief and said, 'Oh, my heart!' and 'One of these days!' and Ruth, giving Lindy a gentle tickle in the ribs, said, 'You mean gooseberries?'

'Gooseberries *duckberries*,' said Lindy, and began to roar with laughter. 'Gooseberries *duckberries*, my bruvver calls them.'

'Leave her with me,' smiled Ruth. 'I'll give her something to soothe the tummyache and keep an eye on her for a while longer, just to be sure. Then I'll bring her back at home-time and have a word with her mother. Going to stay and play nurses with me, Lindy?'

At three-twenty Ruth and Lindy, holding hands,

strolled over to Pre-prep, where Lindy's mother was already parked in a very dusty Range Rover. Ruth explained about the tummyache and heard about the unripe gooseberries, and Lindy's mother thanked her very much and said if it didn't clear up they'd go down to Dr Gather's surgery anyway, just to be sure. Ruth smiled goodbye and went to see Miss Decker. Some prospective parents were in her study and Ruth was introduced. She had hoped to pursue that previous conversation about the Gather children, but clearly Miss Decker was going to be tied up for some while.

Ruth walked back by the tennis-courts, where Angus, his right arm in a sling, was coaching some seniors. He gave her a wave and she stopped to watch for a moment or two, then headed for the swimming-pool, where she paused for a while and thought how delicious the water looked, how innocently inviting, and what happy little fishes the children were as they swam and dived with careless ease.

That night there was an incident at supper when some hot soup got spilled, but this was dealt with very sensibly by one of the teachers on duty, who had already applied the cold water treatment before Ruth arrived on the scene. No need for Dr Gather again.

But the tree incident was a different matter. And afterwards Ruth was to say to herself that could she not just have taken a bet on it? Trust Danny to make the end of her first term—and her birthday—so memorable!

It happened just before three o'clock in the afternoon.

Pre-prep had closed at midday, Rosie Gather going home with Olivia May for lunch. Most of the boarders had already left, some for Bristol airport escorted by teachers, the majority collected by mothers driving family cars with boots big enough to take trunks and sports gear and teddy bears. Dr Gather had left a message with Danny's housemaster that he would be there by three-fifteen. So Danny and his pals had stationed themselves by the entrance to the drive where they could see their parents' cars turn in at the school gates. Boys being boys, they had not been content to hang about on terra firma. So they had climbed into the trees.

It was Ruth's birthday. But she had been too busy even to collect her mail from the office, let alone give much thought to the significance of the day.

At two fifty-seven precisely Danny fell.

He wasn't more than twelve feet up. But it was a clumsy sort of crash-landing through whippy green branches, in the process of which a sharp twig got him right in the mouth. 'Ugggggghhhh!' shrieked Danny, tumbling in a heap of thrashing limbs on to a bouncy cushion of leaf mould. The other two came scrambling down to join him, their faces ghastly till they saw their friend still alive and kicking, struggling to his feet and turning towards them.

Andy was almost sick. 'Ugghh!' he shuddered in an echo of Danny's own injured wail.

'Phew, man, you should see yourself!' Julian, bravest of the three, reached to pull out the twig which stuck grotesquely through Danny's purple, swollen lower lip.

'Naaah!' Danny reared back as the pain became agonising. Speaking was almost impossible, but he made it very obvious he didn't relish any amateur first aid.

'Andy!' said Julian urgently. 'Come on, will you? Get hold of Danny's arm. We gotta get him to Silkey quick before all his blood runs out of him!'

The bleeding was indeed awesome. Danny could feel it falling in great warm blobs on to his clean grey shirt, his mouth puffing and throbbing as he was rushed woolly-legged through the shrubbery taking the unofficial short cut to the san.

Ruth, with Richard Harrison's father, was standing by the art display, together admiring the Tolkien painting. 'Never any good at art myself,' said Mr Harrison. 'Much preferred woodwork.'

Mr Harrison was an orthopod, Ruth remembered. 'Which is your hospital?' she asked him.

'Royal Hanoverian,' came the response. 'After Epsom College, Richard's hoping to do medicine at the Hanoverian—unless you've changed your mind, young man, and decided to follow in Picasso's footsteps?' Mr Harrison's hearty laughter ceased as the dishevelled trio came gasping into the hall.

'Danny!' groaned Sister Silke. 'Whatever next?' To the boys' ears, she sounded more than a trifle vexed.

Just like Dad, shivered Danny.

'Into the treatment-room,' she ordered. 'No, not you two. You go to the main office and ask them to ring Dr Gather.'

The boys explained that they were waiting for the doctor at the gate when Danny fell from the tree. Hearing this, Ruth sent them off to intercept him.

'Anything I can do?' offered Mr Harrison.

'That's very kind of you, but this is Dr Gather's son and his father should be here any moment—apparently.

Goodbye, Richard, and thank you again for letting me keep your painting. All the best for the future. Goodbye, Mr Harrison. Safe journey.'

They left and Ruth went straight to Danny's side. Taking his head between her two cool hands, she surveyed the injury. Poor boy, it did look nasty. 'Falling out of trees, is it, eh? And did you think you were second cousin to a monkey?' she teased gently. 'Now how are you going to give me a birthday kiss with a lip like that?'

She unfastened his ruined tie and threw it aside. 'Let's have that messy shirt off. There. Hop up on the couch and let's see if we can clean you up before Daddy comes to put in a few tiny stitches.'

Experimentally she touched the protruding twig. The boy flinched, even though she had hardly hurt him. 'Danny, I think if you lie down it'll make it easier for me to get at you. Look at the pictures I've stuck on the ceiling and see if you can work out the puzzle.'

Local anaesthetic, suturing equipment, dressings, size eight surgical gloves . . . As she laid up the trolley Ruth carried on a flow of cheerful chatter. 'I once fell out of a tree, you know. I was about your age too. But I fell on my father and broke his glasses. He was none too pleased. It was an apple tree, I seem to remember. We used to have a hammock and I loved to lie in it and read. Do you like reading, Danny?'

He shook his head. His face was white and sweaty. 'You don't? No, I guess you wouldn't, Mr Action Man. Doesn't your daddy read to you at bedtime?'

'Sometimes. He used to.' It was painful for Danny to speak, and the words were far from clear.

Ruth's gloved hands ripped open a disposable pack

containing gauze, cotton wool, forceps, a small tray. The gallipot she filled with chlorhexidine.

'Now, Danny, will you let me see if I can get this twig out myself or would you prefer me to wait for your father?'

A deep voice, very close by, murmured low instructions. 'Go ahead. It doesn't look too complicated.'

Danny reached out a loving grimy hand and his eyes filled with fresh tears as his father swamped it in his own. 'OK, Danny boy, let's see how hard you can squeeze my hand . . . Hey, call that a squeeze? It's just a little tickle, I can hardly feel anything. Now *that*'s more like it. Yes, I can feel that . . . ouch! You're a real toughie, Danny Gather.'

'There!' exclaimed the nurse triumphantly, holding the bloodstained offender aloft in her forceps. 'See the wretched twig, Danny? All out now and clean as a whistle.' She swapped forceps for cotton swabs and leaned over the couch, steadying the boy's tremulous chin with her fingers, giving him gentle warning, 'I'm going to clean you up with some antiseptic and it's likely to sting a bit, so give me a nod when you're ready . . .' Brave as he was, Danny couldn't help but whimper, and his big brown eyes swam with unshed tears. He had had almost as much as he could take. 'I'm sorry, pet,' whispered Ruth, remembering with an awful pang that there was no mum waiting outside to give the poor kid a warm cuddle when his ordeal was over.

Behind her she heard the snap of latex as Dan put on surgical gloves and reached for the hypodermic which Ruth, anticipating his requirements with cool-headed expertise, had prepared and set ready on the trolley.

While Dan wasn't looking Ruth pressed a warm kiss on the boy's damp cheek, out of sight of his father. She didn't say anything, but her eyes smiled down on him with something in their blue depths that instinctively the child clung to, following her intently as she stepped back and to the side, giving place to the doctor. But Dan nodded to her to come close and hold his sons's hands in case the child should flinch as he put the lignocaine in.

As if there'd never been a cross word between them, they waited in quiet companionship, shoulder to shoulder, for the local anaesthetic to take effect.

Ruth had Blu-tacked puzzle pictures to the ceiling to distract her young patients from their discomfort. 'See, Danny? You have to work out who's going to get through the maze to reach the Gingerbread House. Is it the witch or is it Hansel and Gretel?'

'The witch,' mumbled Danny indistinctly. Gently but firmly Ruth held his hands out of the way while Dan took up the suturing needle and with deft accuracy inserted three fine stitches into the torn lower lip. At his nod, Ruth cut each silk stitch close to the skin. Dan straightened up with a sigh of relief; Danny had been very brave. 'There you are, Danny—good as new! Those stitches will dissolve and there'll hardly be a mark to show for it.'

'You'll be as handsome as ever,' smiled Ruth, taking a can of special plastic surgical spray from her trolley. 'Now I'm going to squirt your stitches with magic invisible skin——'

Danny was sitting up now and the colour was coming

back into his pale cheeks. 'I think I better have a bandage,' he interrupted anxiously.

'*Please*,' reminded his father with what Ruth felt to be unnecessary severity, considering the circumstances.

'Bandage? Certainly, sir!' She opened a fresh sterile pack and—making a solemn ceremony of it—taped a small dressing into place.

'I want to stay with Si-Si-Sister Silke tonight.'

'Don't we all,' muttered his father out of the corner of his mouth, eyeing Ruth very significantly as he rolled down his shirt sleeves and reached for the discarded jacket of his summerweight suit.

Ruth choked, but managed to turn it into an authentic-sounding cough. No way was she going to give Dan the satisfaction of guessing that she wouldn't exactly kick him out of bed! She raised a coolly indifferent eyebrow and Dan responded with a full frontal grin that turned her weak at the knees and threatened to reduce her hauteur to giggles.

He gathered up the limp seven-year-old into his arms, and the curly head nestled wearily into his shoulder. 'Sister's on holiday as from now,' he told his son. '*I'm* going to nurse you tonight, so it's home, James, and straight to bed.'

'My name's not James,' protested Danny indistinctly, making both nurse and doctor smile.

'Look,' said Ruth, 'I'd be more than happy to keep Danny here for the night. If there's a problem at home——'

'No problem. Bea's out on the razzle with her boyfriend—they're going to an organ recital in Wells Cathedral. Rosie's sleeping round at one of her friends', so I shall devote my entire self to tending my wounded soldier. Eh, Danny? How d'you like that?'

There was nothing Danny would like better. Ruth knew *that*.

Dr Gather seemed in no hurry to go. He was looking at her as if there was something else he very much wanted to say, but was unsure how to go about it. Ruth felt perplexed. Dan, who was always so much in command of any given situation . . . what could it be? Something that could not be said in front of the child?

She experienced a sudden anxiety. It must be to do with her work, some criticism. Ah—the Arrangement! That was it. Dr Gather didn't fancy the idea of Sister Silke staying in his home.

His voice broke across her thoughts. 'Well, we must let you get on with your packing. I take it you're going away?'

Ruth didn't hesitate but replied quickly that yes, she was going to Birmingham for a few days, and then to Devon to see her mother. Rather stilted goodbyes were exchanged. Then Danny flung out an arm to her and lifted his face to give her a kiss. The pad on his lower lip got in the way, but Ruth squeezed his hot sticky hand.

She went to open the main door for Dan as he carried his son to the car, then she hurried back to restore the treatment-room to apple-pie order. She felt hurt, and strangely sore inside. Perhaps the research trip to New Orleans was off? In which case Bea Gather might have rung! she thought indignantly as, with vigorous movements, she wiped down the trolley. It would have been the considerate thing to do, to let her know she wasn't going to be needed, after all, during those three

August weeks that Bea was to have gone away.

Behind Ruth's back the door opened.

Two strong hands caught hold of her by the waist and swung her round. Her plastic apron rasped against dark-blue Aquascutum cool-wool.

It happened too quickly for Ruth to feel any fear. Rather a sense of astonishment and disbelief when it was all over. And an overwhelming desire to go through the whole process again; and in ultra-slow motion, so that this time it wouldn't seem like a dream . . .

CHAPTER TEN

'HAPPY BIRTHDAY!' murmured Dan, releasing Ruth. The next moment, seeing the shocked nurse sway dangerously on unsteady feet, he reached out a hasty hand to grasp hold of her arm. It had been a daft thing to do, creeping up on the poor girl like that.

'Danny was sad he couldn't give you a proper birthday kiss—so I volunteered to do the job for him.'

Ruth was knocked speechless. What could she possibly say? Thank you was hardly appropriate. And now Dan was taking a good look at what he had so rashly kissed, and evidently wishing he hadn't bothered.

She just stood there, cloth in one hand, bottle of disinfectant in the other. There was a puddle of spilled green liquid on the floor and the room reeked of hospitals. How her apron had crackled as their bodies collided! And was that thundering noise in her ears really just the sound of her own heartbeats?

'I'll be seeing you,' he said, and now he wasn't smiling. 'Take care of yourself.' Ruth was aware of the pressure of his fingers tightening momentarily, then her arm was free and he was gone.

The first thing she did was rush to the mirror and stare at her breathless reflection, trying to see herself through Dan's eyes. Her hair was dangling to her shoulders, soft and fluffy from the morning shower and much in need of a brisk pair of scissors; her eyes glittered and the whites were very white, her cheeks and her full lips very pink. She did actually look quite pretty, for her, if somewhat dishevelled. And her cap was falling off the back of her head.

She pulled it back into place and rammed in the white hairpins.

There was plenty to occupy her for the rest of the day as she sorted and tidied and checked and re-ordered; finally switching off the computer and locking offices and medical-rooms, but leaving the ward open for the cleaners who would be coming in during the holidays. The geraniums were flowering magnificently. But they couldn't be left untended, so Ruth grouped the pots in a great splash of colour on the front step where the gardener had promised to water them.

By the time she remembered her birthday post—her mind was so obsessed with Dan—it was late and Admin was locked. But she borrowed a key and in the wire tray marked 'Staff' found a bulky packet from her mother and several first-class letters, one in large black handwriting which she opened and read as she strolled back to the san to make her supper.

Ditchingham House was strangely silent; most of the staff owned small properties in other parts of the country, where they headed once term was over. Several families with young children had gone to bed early, their cars loaded to the roof-racks, planning an early start on quiet roads to make for the cross-channel ferries and camping sites in France. Ruth saw no one, and her birthday went unnoted and unremarked. She didn't mind. It wasn't as if, she told herself, she had anyone to celebrate with. Her second birthday since Jeff had died.

The contents of the letter in her hand had a decidedly cheerful tone. Ruth could read it clearly without her glasses, for Suzie wrote with a black felt-tipped pen and the invitation shot off the page.

'Have a day on me,' Suzie urged, 'at Peasdowne Place. All the beauty treatments you can cram in. Come as soon as you can. Come tomorrow! Dan tells me it's end of term.'

'Dan tells me' . . . Three little words that turned Ruth stone-cold sober. How could she have forgotten what sort of man he was? How could she have let her guard slip?

There was worse to come. 'Just give me a buzz and I'll tell you what gear you need to bring. See you! Luv, Suzie. PS. Isn't all this sun sun sun absolutely glorious? I'm going to Italy mid-August, and not alone, needless to say. Great news, by the way. Maybe you can guess!'

Suspicion confirmed, Ruth's expression was tragic as she let herself back into the empty san.

She had slumped in front of the television to watch *Coronation Street*, which she hadn't caught up with for weeks. Then her mother rang and sang 'Happy Birthday, dear Ruth,' in a very jolly soprano. And since she had her hand on the phone Ruth succumbed to a sudden urge and dialled Suzie there and then: bright-as-a-button Suzie, on a permanent high because she was in love with her job and her man. 'Come first thing,' she urged, 'eight o'clock if you can make it. We'll have breakfast together, just the two of us, and you can tell me all your news and I'll let you in on my big secret.'

A secret which was bound to involve Dr Daniel Gather.

Oh, why have I let myself in for this? agonised Ruth as she put the receiver down. I'm going to have to put on a pretty good act when Suzie tells me. I'm going to have to smile and pretend I couldn't be happier for both of them.

She switched off the television and padded barefoot into the bedroom to sort her things out for the early start, edging round the bed to draw the curtains, then pausing for a moment, elbows on the sill, captivated by the dramatic beauty of the darkening apricot sky.

You'll get over it, Ruth, she told herself optimistically. You're a tough lady, a survivor. You can get over anything.

And I can certainly get over you, Dan Gather! One kiss does not a love-affair make.

She was still thinking about Dan as she drove along the country lanes, heading for Peasdowne. The sky was a flawless Mediterranean blue. The grassy verges looked as if they could do with some rain.

This wretched uncertainty surrounding the Arrangement was really getting to Ruth. Especially after what Suzie had said. If she was going to be needed to babysit, then they had better decide pretty damn quick; because if Dan and Suzie were off to Italy and Bea *was* off to New Orleans to research background for her latest book, then he sure as hell was going to need someone to take care of Rosie and Danny, and since she had already been stupid enough to commit herself, she was going to have to grin and bear it. But it was going to be pretty awful, being there alone in Dan's house with his children, while he was off gallivanting with Suzie.

Forget the man! ordered her sensible inner self. Enjoy yourself. It's not every nurse who gets the chance to visit a health farm.

Mmm . . . true!

She had always felt a sneaking desire to be pampered at a place like Peasdowne. It must be something to do with nursing: a bit of glamour, a bit of spoiling . . . last on a nurse's list of priorities, for there was neither the time nor the money. At least she would get her hair cut.

'We've got a great hairdresser here,' Suzie had enthused. 'Sure, she'll fix your hair for you. You won't recognise yourself, Ruth, we'll do your make-up and everything. Bring a nice dress to wear home. Bring a bikini and wear a tracksuit.'

'A tracksuit? I don't own a tra——'

'No problem. Shorts and T-shirt are just as good. Ask for me at reception and you'll get the VIP works. Must dash.'

So Ruth was wearing her new white shorts and peach T-shirt, and her silk underwear. She wore no make-up and her hair was scooped into a high bouncy ponytail. Her thighs on the car seat looked horribly white and substantial.

Ruth had been told to keep an eye out on the left-hand side for the Peasdowne entrance. Here it was! Her sandalled foot hit the brake and she changed gear, steering the Metro under a Gothic arch of glossy black wrought-iron, tyres crunching on the change of surface as she began to follow a snaking white drive which disappeared over the crest of the distant hill. On either side stretched the grassy parklands of a once-great estate, and in the shade of ancient oak and spreading chestnut trees grazed a herd of fallow deer, lifting their elegant heads to stare wary-eyed as Ruth drove slowly past.

Beyond the gentle green slopes Peasdowne Place came into view, grand and stately, quite dwarfing Ditchingham House. Ruth gave a gasp at first sight of it. 'Good grief!' she said out loud. 'Dan comes over here to play *tennis*?'

She parked her dusty little car in the shadow of an ivory Rolls Royce with the number-plates TOP 1, heaved her small canvas bag out of the back seat and started gamely up a flight of marble steps, still slippery with the morning dew.

A pair of snarling lions offered a stony welcome at the great front door. It was wide open, so Ruth walked straight in and found herself in the entrance hall. The air smelled of beeswax polish and fresh flowers. Great gilded mirrors reflected light from the windows and sunshine streamed in through the open doors, surrounding her in a golden halo as she paused to get her bearings.

'Miss Silke?' enquired a voice with a smile in it.

Ruth turned her head to see a reception desk with two telephones and a computer with VDU. A blonde girl with spectacles was rising to her feet and extending a hand in welcome. 'You're expected, Miss Silke. If you care to take a seat I'll buzz Sister Lake and let her know you're here.'

Before Ruth could correct her about the 'Miss', the blonde beamed her smile upon another enquirer waiting at Ruth's elbow. Anyway, it didn't seem important.

Ruth perched gingerly on a fragile gilt chair that looked as if Marie Antoinette had sat on it last. A man and woman in damp white bathrobes—they had evidently been for a pre-breakfast swim—came padding through the hall in thonged rubber flip-flops. Others wearing all manner of *déshabillé*—tracksuits, leotards—strolled up to the desk to check their individual programmes on the computer screen. They glanced in Ruth's direction and murmured friendly hellos. 'My last day,' said one woman gleefully, seeing that Ruth had just arrived, 'and I'm nine pounds down. I feel like a bird!'

Ruth nodded and smiled and gazed about her, fascinated by it all. Everyone she saw looked happy and casual and relaxed, the lines of stress wiped from their faces, no frowns, no bad temper, no hassle. Whatever, she wondered in secret amusement, did the noble ghosts of Peasdowne make of such goings-on within their historic home?

'Ruth!' echoed a dramatic voice from somewhere in the gods—and there, poised on the turn of the great staircase, was Suzie.

Beaming all over her face, Ruth sprang to her feet and, forgetting her bag, rushed to greet her as she came briskly down the stairs, slender and svelte in white with touches of dramatic black.

Suzie too had grown her hair. But hers was expertly cut in a longer version of her swinging fringed bob and she looked more Cleopatra-like than ever. Her white dress with its short sleeves and open revers was similar in style to Ruth's usual uniform; but this contour-skimming version had been made to measure in an expensive silky cotton, the narrow skirt baring Suzie's elegant knees. Her belt was black grosgrain, with a large and elaborate antique silver buckle. Several nursing badges decorated the breast of her dress and she wore pale silk stockings and black suede Charles Jourdan shoes with high slender heels.

Only Suzie could make a sister's outfit look so devastatingly chic! said Ruth to herself admiringly. She saw that very same admiration reflected in the eyes of the girl on the reception desk, in the upturned faces of the guests. And the recognition followed right on cue, with a secret, private pain that shocked and surprised her: Dan Gather and Suzie Lake were destined for each other. Like attracted to like. Yes, oh yes, it had to be faced: Suzie Lake and Daniel Gather were the perfect match . . . and Ruth, with poor Miss Decker, was just another admirer in the wings.

They breakfasted in Suzie's suite of rooms, where, after a quick résumé of the summer term at Ditchingham House, it was Ruth's turn to listen. She hadn't been far off the mark about the extent of the nursing duties: Suzie was now much more of an administrator, and answerable to Sybille Jardyne, the owner of Peasdowne, who retained her own wing of the great house, and was often abroad. Most of the organisation was left to her son Edward, who had a Harvard Business School degree, and was Suzie's immediate boss.

'Don't you envy me?' sparkled Suzie. 'I really have

fallen on my feet——'

'I certainly do,' agreed Ruth, with more tact than honesty.

'And it's all thanks to *darling* Dan——'

Here it comes, thought Ruth, steeling herself to keep smiling. Now she's going to tell me . . . 'This is delicious!' she interrupted hurriedly, staving off Suzie's big news for a few seconds longer. 'I've never eaten Greek yoghurt before. So thick and creamy . . .'

'Try a dollop of this honey with it. It's from our own bees. We grow all our own vegetables by organic methods, and we've our own Jersey herd. The muesli's home-made too. And, of course, freshly squeezed orange juice.'

'From your own orange groves?' chuckled Ruth, long accustomed to concealing a heavy heart.

'Well may you laugh, but we're working on it. You have yet to see our Orangery. That's a sort of huge garden-room full of orange trees growing in tubs,' Suzie explained in answer to Ruth's blank look. 'More coffee, Sister?'

'*Thank* you, Sister.' They exchanged grins.

'This is all pretty swish,' observed Ruth, admiring Suzie's elegant suite of rooms. 'Are you the boss lady around here?'

'Not *quite*,' came the arch response, 'but I am responsible for managing the health side of the business. As you'll see, we function like a luxury hotel, skimping on nothing. But Peasdowne places great emphasis on health promotion and illness prevention. Each client has a thorough medical check-up and an individual programme of treatments—oh, yes, *you* too. You want to know what's in store? Well, you'll be weighed and measured and your medical history will be noted. Usually we ask if people have come to rest or to lose weight. We have an anti-stress programme for businessmen—or women,' Suzie added, seeing Ruth was about to. 'I've prepared a schedule in advance for you, with the emphasis on beauty treatments this afternoon and exercising this morning. How does that sound?'

'Exercising? So I'm to be put on the rack and tortured?'

'Don't knock it till you've tried it,' laughed Suzie, lighting up her first cigarette of the day. 'I know, but I'm making a real effort to cut down ... By the way, I haven't booked you for the low-calorie restaurant because you don't need to lose any weight.'

Ruth pinched a firm bare thigh and looked rueful.

'You're tall and well in proportion,' insisted the expert firmly. 'And after a term of school food you deserve a really special lunch. It's à la carte and on the house. Oh, and tonight I want you to have dinner with Edward Jardyne. And me, of course, and ... mmm ... one or two others. Did you bring a dress? Let me have it and I'll get it pressed and hung up for you to change into this evening.'

'You're being tremendously kind to me!' Ruth managed faintly. 'I'd no idea ...'

Suzie reached across and squeezed her hand. 'My birthday present—albeit a day late.'

Ruth gaped. 'H-how did you know?'

'Little bird!' Suzie tapped the side of her nose with a crimson fingernail.

Immediately Ruth felt guilty and accused herself of being mean-spirited. Here she was, doing her best to postpone the sharing of Suzie's happiness. And Suzie so kind and generous on her part. Ruth took a deep breath and braced herself. 'Suzie—you were going to tell me—you know, you said you had something . . .'

A mysterious grin was her answer. 'Wait till tonight. Now, let's get going. I've another surprise in store for you.'

'Great!' Ruth said happily, draining her coffee-cup and picking up her canvas bag. 'Lead on, Macduff!'

'Fifty-nine kilos—that's nine stone four to you,' said Nurse Sarah, noting Ruth's height and weight on the consultation forms. 'Excellent.'

'Have you got any disappearing cream for hips?' joked Ruth.

The nurse cast an experienced eye over Ruth's figure, comprehensively revealed by last summer's strapless pink bikini. 'Nothing wrong with your hips, my dear. You've what used to be known as an hour-glass figure. Curves are back in fashion. And you've a nice flat tummy. The gymnast will teach you some exercises to tighten your thigh muscles, but I wouldn't advise actual weight loss.

'Now, if you wouldn't mind going behind the screens and slipping your top off—there's a paper gown on the couch—Doctor will be with you in just a moment. I'll go and tell him you're ready.'

Ruth did as she was told, lying down flat and wriggling her toes to exercise the circulation, quite relaxed, her hands clasped on her paper gown—a mite short for a tall girl, reaching only to mid-thigh, they'd used longer ones at the Shotover Clinic—pleasantly anticipating the day ahead.

What would this 'surprise' turn out to be? She did hope they didn't plan to turn her into a cropped redhead!

She heard a door open, a telephone begin ringing in the distance and the nurse's voice say quickly, 'I'll answer that.' Then the sound of a man's firm tread crossing to where Ruth lay supine behind the curtains, her features composed in a polite smile of greeting.

The curtain swished aside.

'Good morning!' said a gleeful Dan, rubbing his hands together as if on this July morning they might be rather chilly. Or perhaps he specially relished the gasp of dismay escaping from his captive colleague.

He was wearing a white coat—something which he never did when working with the children—and his shirt was pale blue with a fine pink stripe, his bow-tie of palest pink silk. He had a stethoscope in his hand and looked as wickedly assured and confident as ever.

Not a trace of surprise, noted Ruth bitterly, getting to grips with her initial shock. Not in the least intimidated by her furious scowl. Absolutely in control of the situation. As ever. Typical Dr Dan!

She sat up, arms folded in a barrier against him.

'What are you doing here?' she demanded, suspicious that she was the victim of some practical joke.

'I'm doing a locum,' said Dan evenly. 'The medical officer is on holiday with his family. He happens to be a friend of mine. Would you mind taking that thing off?'

'You must be joking!'

Ruth swung her legs over the side of the couch, displaying a swift glimpse of her pink bikini pants.

'I see we match,' grinned Dan, fingering his bow-tie. 'What do you think? Bea's choice, as ever. I've very little interest in clothes—mine, that is. Now, can I see you without yours?'

Ruth actually swore. 'No, you . . . can't!' she snapped.

'Spoilsport,' Dan sighed amiably. 'It would make things easier for me, but not to worry. Now let's start with your blood pressure.'

Ruth submitted with ill grace. On the receiving end, she decided it was actually quite unpleasant having your arm pumped up till it felt about to burst.

'One-sixty over a hundred.' Dan raised an eyebrow. 'Dear, dear! I hope it's just the shock and delight of my sudden proximity. The heart-stopping surprise of seeing me.'

'Surprise?' repeated Ruth grimly. 'You're a surprise all right!' Oh, so that was it! Dan himself was the promised surprise. He and Suzie had fixed it between them. 'You and Suzie planned this,' she said bitterly.

'Shh!' he reprimanded. 'Nurse will be back any moment.' He reached for her chest with his stethoscope, tugged down the paper neckline. 'Dear, dear, dear! This is dreadful.' His face frowned at her in mock-severity, but his eyes held an undisguisedly sensual gleam. Ruth saw it and was shocked to find her body reacting while her rational self resisted. The physical response was almost uncontrollable. Her limbs seemed to drain of blood and to weaken. Her body wanted to fall back on the bed in submission . . .

But she knew her core of steel would not desert her. Under the flimsy gown her shoulders set straight and her backbone stiffened. 'I'm very cross indeed,' she insisted through gritted teeth. 'You won't get any accurate readings from me in the state I'm in. You and your girlfriend——'

The nurse appeared round the screen. 'Sorry about that, Dr Gather. When you've finished here, could you examine a gentleman complaining of chest pains?'

'Certainly,' responded the amiable Dr Gather. 'Stand up, please. Turn around and let me see the backs of your legs. Any problems with the veins? No. You're in fine shape, Miss—er——'

'Miss Silke,' supplied the nurse helpfully. 'Miss Silke has no figure problems. She's here for a day's programme of exercise and beauty treatments.'

The nurse stayed with them for the next five minutes, during which Dan behaved impeccably and pretended he didn't know Ruth from Eve.

Left alone to dress, Ruth sat for a moment on the examination couch deep in thought. Her reaction had been a bit over the top. She'd been a bit silly to get so cross . . .

Suzie and Dan could have no idea how she felt about him. Sure, they must have thought it would be a bit of a lark not to tell her Dan Gather himself would be doing her medical. But they could have no idea how devastating the encounter might prove. It was one thing working with Dan in a professional context, quite another to be confronted by him, disarmed and unsuspecting, in a situation of such intimacy.

All the same, losing her cool like that! How he and Suzie would laugh, at the prim and proper Sister Silke!

CHAPTER ELEVEN

'HAVE you enjoyed your activity programme, Miss Silke?'

All day she had been addressed as *Miss*. She wasn't bothered by their mistake, but all the same Ruth was quite surprised. If Suzie had been told about such a small event as her birthday, wouldn't Dan also have told her about 'poor old Ruth' losing her husband?

A moment's pondering brought Ruth to the conclusion that however close the relationship between Suzie and Dan, this wasn't necessarily so. For you couldn't be a doctor without some sense of compassion for others, and a deal of discretion. And he had been kind and sensitive when she told him about Jeff, for he too had experienced tragedy at first hand.

He did speak of it, briefly, once.

Arriving early, he had found Ruth in the office, reading a newspaper during her lunch break and clearly upset by a tragedy involving post-natal depression. Had she known she would never have shown him the report.

Dan had then spoken of his own loss, factually and without emotion. His wife had killed herself after Rosie's birth. It was an overdose, and post-natal depression was the coroner's verdict.

Why? Ruth's stricken eyes had put the question her lips had feared to form.

The explanation was terse, and grim. Rosie had been born by Caesarian section requiring general anaesthesia. Juliette had interpreted this as failure; she'd grieved because she did not see her daughter born, suffered grief and disappointment over not experiencing a vaginal delivery. 'Not uncommon,' Dan had said wearily, avoiding Ruth's face. 'It's a major op going deep into the stomach at a time when a woman is extremely emotional. That fact tends to get glossed over.'

He had sought no consolation from Ruth—it was a tragedy he had learned to live with—and he had moved quickly on to medical matters.

She had only worked with him for one fascinating term, but that was quite long enough to see how unfailingly kind and caring Dan was with his young patients. And she had come to see that his assessment of his son's needs, while practical in the circumstances, was both loving and valid. She could admit it now; she had perhaps over-reacted in her first professional concern for a seemingly accident-prone child.

The blonde on the desk had been replaced by a tall redhead who bore a passing resemblance to Marti Caine. 'Miss Silke?' the girl prompted, rousing Ruth from her blue study. 'Are you all right?'

Ruth shook herself and assured the girl that she was fine, that she had had a simply marvellous day.

'We're so glad! Now,' suggested the redhead, 'if you'd care to wait in Miss Lake's apartment?'

The telephone rang in Suzie's sitting-room. Ruth wondered if she should answer it. It was so persistent that she finally did so, and heard Suzie's crisp voice on the line.

'I'm in the boutique and I've found a sensational dress you can borrow for the dinner-dance tonight. Come down right away and try it on.'

'Suzie?' Ruth's voice was puzzled.

Suzie was a mind-reader. 'No, dear, yours is a nice dress, but not *quite* right for Gala Night.'

Oh, God! sighed Ruth. She's going to dress me up and make an exhibition of me when all I'll want to do is fade into the wallpaper when she tells me about their engagement.

A little sigh escaped her lips. It was likely that Dan would be there, as well as this Edward Jardyne. She must look good, to help herself act brave.

She lifted her chin. 'I'll be right down.'

The morning had flown by, one exhilarating session following another, never a moment to be bored. There had been facials, and heat and massage treatments, and a wax bath in which Ruth lay on a couch wearing just a triangle of gauze and an anxious expression, on tenterhooks in case Dan Gather should come sauntering by. Expert hands covered her entire body with paraffin wax, heated and whisked to a frothy foam; then they wrapped her in cloths and blankets and left her to sweat till the wax had solidified into a white shell. The shower afterwards was just bliss, and already her skin looked polished and perfect as marble.

After that was a jazz-dance class at which Ruth displayed a talent she never knew she had, responding supplely and instinctively to the rhythm of the beat. She lunched in a borrowed dressing-gown with a group of other women she had met in the women's sauna; and the whole afternoon was taken up with beauty treatments and a manicure and hairdo. The manicure she frankly felt was a waste of time, since her nails had to be kept short and she refused the bright colours she was offered. But the clever girl won her round with a Dior polish called Très Pâle, a transparent milky shade, which looked very good, especially after the treatment they had used to soften and whiten Ruth's workaday hands.

In her heart of hearts, Ruth thought the make-up artist wielded too dramatic a brush. But after her initial impulse to reach for the cleansing cream she settled down to enjoying her taste of glamour. It was too sophisticated by far: the eye make-up was fantastic really, blended like a butterfly's wing, and the deep bronze lipstick not at all her usual choice of shade, but flattering to say the least.

Best of all was her hair. The stylist must have had magic scissors.

First they used a camomile shampoo to bring out the fairness, and a real egg for conditioning. Then the stylist took ages, cutting short feathery layers so her hair seemed to spring from her scalp in soft curls, revealing the neat whorls of her ears and the long line of her pale neck.

Suzie at any rate was well satisfied. 'You look beautiful,' she said simply, then leant forward and kissed Ruth's surprised cheek. 'I am glad you came,' she went on. 'I could see you'd be stunning if we just showed you how.'

I hope this will stay put for a couple of hours, thought Ruth wistfully. And the thought translated itself into words. 'Is Dr Gather going to be here tonight?' she heard herself asking.

'Of course.'

Suzie lowered her lashes and her Paloma Red mouth smiled secretively. She was wearing silver tonight: very short and moulded to her body; a strapless shimmering sheath which, when she turned round, revealed a startlingly bare back and a huge glittering bow decorating the base of her spine.

'How will you sit down?' wondered Ruth.

'Goodness knows!' was the careless reply.

Ruth had let herself be coaxed into black rather than her usual pastel prints. Suzie was formidably bossy and Ruth did as she was told, aware she was right out of her depth. She had gone doubtfully to the boutique to find Suzie holding up against herself the sort of frivolous creation that Ruth would never have dreamed of wearing in a month of Sundays. 'Try this one,' Suzie ordered. 'I've got a feeling about this one.'

Definitely not me! was Ruth's immediate reaction. But lately she had been proved wrong about so many things that she was beginning to mistrust her own judgement. 'Sensational!' was Suzie's satisfied verdict.

'If you say so,' murmured Ruth, quite awed by the sight of this unfamiliar stranger showing so much leg and the rest.

'Black tights,' ordered Suzie, tossing her a pack from the display. 'And those black shoes you've brought with you will do well enough, though I'd personally have gone for a really high heel.'

The dress was a black silk sheath ending well above the knee. But more than that. It was topped by a wide off-the-shoulder frill of fuchsia-pink satin, repeated at the waist to form a mini-overskirt. 'We'll have to change your lipstick,' said Suzie, and that seemed to settle that. 'I can't lend you a strapless bra, I'm nowhere near as big as you, but the fit's superb and you should be OK. Dan'll just love it!'

That was not a tactful remark. Ruth's eyelids fluttered down to hide the puzzled hurt in her eyes.

She was whisked back to the salon for her lipstick to be redone. The beautician chose a deep wine colour and mixed some bright pink into the peacock mix on her eyelids. And it looked marvellous!

You live and learn! muttered Ruth, eyeing her astonishing reflection. Oh, Dan, if only you'd look at me tonight and forget Suzie exists! She could have any man she wants. Why must she want mine?

The face in the glass looked back at her, aghast and penitent, the glossy lips parting in breathless shame. He's *not* yours, an inner voice said scornfully. Dan Gather's not a thing to be owned. You've lived without a man for two years. You don't need a man, you're a professional woman with a worthwhile job and well able to take care of yourself. You're twenty-six . . . no, twenty-seven! Satisfaction in life doesn't depend on any Prince Charming. And you know perfectly well: Dan Gather's more Don Giovanni than Prince Charles.

'If you're not happy with it, I'll try something different,' said the beautician, concerned by Ruth's fixed solemnity.

'It's wonderful . . .' whispered Ruth sadly.

The wing that housed the Jardynes was enough to make Ruth's eyes pop at the unashamed luxury of it all. Sybille Jardyne had employed a top interior decorator and her drawing-room was a symphony in ivory against which the dark wood of the Jacobean panelling glowed. Ruth's heels sank into inches of creamy carpet and she hoped to goodness her soles were clean. She was feeling very tense. Any moment now, Dan would be joining them. Mrs Jardyne was away, holidaying on Mustique. 'Dan shouldn't be late,' remarked Suzie, in the know. 'He hasn't got to put the kids to bed tonight.'

'What can I get you ladies to drink?' asked Edward. His accent was tinged with New York, where he'd worked, after Harvard, for several years.

Ruth hesitated. Should she request some exotic cocktail or was it all right to ask for sherry?

'Have a Kir,' suggested Suzie, and Ruth nodded.

'For us both, darling,' drawled Suzie.

Ruth was feeling increasingly uncomfortable. The way Suzie had introduced her had rung the warning bells. Why was everyone so keen these days to fix her up with a man? 'Edward,' Suzie had murmured, 'here,' she'd said significantly, 'is Ruth.' As if Ruth had been acquired that afternoon in the slave market and dolled up for the master's pleasure! With sinking heart Ruth saw the pattern of the evening. Dan and Suzie. Edward got the consolation prize: Ruth.

'So you're the lady most likely to——' said Edward, taking her hand and studying her with narrowed eyes.

Suzie stopped his words by laying an intimate finger on his lips. '*En avance*,' she murmured, and her long black hair swished about her shoulders with the warning shake of her head.

What on earth was going on? mused a very puzzled Ruth. Most likely to what? To take over here when Suzie moved in with Dr Gather? No, it couldn't possibly be that. The very thought was ridiculous.

Suzie was flirting outrageously. Those two hardly seemed able to keep their hands off each other!

Ruth eyed Edward Jardyne covertly. Indeed he wasn't tall, and he wasn't good-looking. But there was something peculiarly fascinating about the man. The sort of charisma that must have drawn Jackie Kennedy to Aristotle Onassis.

Edward and Suzie had now linked arms and were gazing raptly into each other's eyes. Any moment Dan would arrive. Suzie was behaving very badly. But she looked so beautiful that you couldn't blame Mr Jardyne for being mesmerised.

'Dr Gather,' announced the maid, entering the room.

Suzie and Edward remained entwined. Ruth saw Dan's tall figure fill the doorway and her heart turned over. Suzie must be mad!

If Dan was angry then he controlled it well, pausing on the threshold as with an ominous half-smile he surveyed the scene. He was carrying a magnum of champagne which he handed over to the maid, who removed herself to a discreet distance.

In evening dress he was once more the formidable stranger, his height and his darkness alien and impressive in the cool, pale, sumptuous room. Yet he was not the stranger he seemed. Ruth had grown to know him so well; that way he had of looking at her without smiling, the heavy-lidded speculative expression, the sensuous furl of his lower lip. How the shivers ran down her spine when he looked at her that way, as he was doing now. How familiar the wavy lock of hair which tended to fall forward over his forehead, the curls at the nape of his neck.

Dan was kissing Suzie now, and she was turning her head, offering her cheek so that her lipstick shouldn't be spoiled. Ruth could only stand and watch anxiously, with unselfconscious concern.

Suzie's eyes glittered strangely as she watched Dan move to Ruth's side and lower his head politely to kiss her too on the cheek.

'Hello, Cinderella,' he murmured softly.

She managed to joke feebly, 'At midnight this turns into my uniform!'

'Take your pulse, Nurse?' Reminding her of the morning's encounter, his voice was low and teasing, for her ears only. She felt his fingers on her wrist and snatched her arm away like an adolescent girl.

'You've cut your hair,' he commented.

'I went out in the rain and it shrank.'

'I thought you were growing it to please me.'

Ruth's eyebrows lifted haughtily. She remembered well enough what he'd said that night in the headmaster's garden. 'I cut it to please *me*. It's a question of looking practical.'

'I don't want you looking practical, I want you looking sexy. You're incredibly sexy tonight.'

Ruth laughed out loud in delight. It was wrong to encourage him, it was dangerous, but he was wonderful.

Dan grinned. He loved her laughter. Their verbal sparring often ended up this way.

'I'm sorry you don't like my hair,' she said mockingly. 'Suzie's grown hers for you.'

'Suzie can shave her head as far as I'm concerned. As it happens, I think your hair's terrific. It suits you extremely well—shows your neck's clean.'

'Oh, you!'

Edward had torn himself away from Suzie and was placing a hand on Dan's sleeve. Ruth came down to earth with a crash. Oh, God, she thought dramatically, were the men going to fight?

Edward winked at Dan.

Dan raised an eyebrow and mouthed, 'Now?'

'Can't think of a better time,' returned Edward, delving into his pocket.

'Right, I'll get the champagne.'

Ruth felt the blood drain from her face. *It was going to be now*! Her fingers began to tremble so badly that she was in danger of spilling her drink all over Mrs Jardyne's ivory carpets.

'I want you, woman,' growled Edward, catching Suzie by her narrow waist and swinging her into position right beneath the crystal chandelier. The glittering light turned her gleaming head to silver. A hand took Ruth's shivering glass away and she was aware of Dan steering her into the circle of light. She stood two feet away and watched, absolutely electrified, as Edward slid an enormous sapphire onto Suzie's engagement finger and—blow the lipstick—took her triumphant body boldly into his arms.

'Bravo!' applauded Dan when the two came up for air. 'My turn . . .'

Suzie slid smoothly into his arms.

For the second time in the space of an hour Ruth had to watch Dan kiss Suzie. But her feelings were very different now.

In a daze of goodwill she admired the sapphire cluster

Suzie was twinkling under her eyes; heard through the ringing in her ears the pop of a champagne cork and the clink of glasses.

Edward looked at the label on the bottle and whistled. 'That's some fine medicine, Doctor!'

'She's worth it.' Dan was looking, though, at Ruth, in all truth finding it hard *not* to look at her, her fair head close to Suzie's black one, her smile delighted and bemused.

'Your big secret! Oh, Suzie, I never dreamed it could be such tremendous news!'

'I know! I was *dying* to tell you at breakfast, but Edward made me wait for Dan. We're going to announce our engagement at dinner; I think the guests will be pleased for us.'

Ruth was making a huge effort to keep her sensible self to the fore. Just because Dr Daniel Gather was behaving as if she were the only woman left on earth, it didn't mean he was about to sweep her up on a white horse and charge off with her into the sunset.

The four of them shared a table in the centre of the dining-room. In the ordinary way, Ruth wouldn't have felt comfortable to be the focus of all eyes; but this was not an ordinary night and she was drunk with pleasure. The mirror told her she looked sensational. And Dan was so tender and attentive; as if in his book she was something very special.

Suzie had given her a few tips on how to eat without ruining her lipstick, but Ruth was too excited under her smooth, sophisticated surface to have any appetite, too thrillingly aware of Dan at her side.

'It may look packed with calories, but it truly isn't,' urged Suzie, concerned to see her friend forcing down tiny portions of scrumptious food.

'You'll fade away,' Dan chided softly, his lips accidentally brushing her ear. Ruth shivered and drank more of that delicious red wine. It tasted of blackcurrants. She had had three glasses already. All she could think about now was kissing Dan—and giving a more responsive performance than she had on her birthday. Her lips throbbed and her eyelids were heavy. His mouth was inches from hers and it would be so easy just to lean across . . .

Some while later, Suzie pushed her chair back. 'Edward and I ought to circulate,' she said. 'Why don't you two go back to the drawing-room for a brandy? We'll meet you there and join the dancing when it's under way.'

I'd better have another black coffee, thought Ruth. I couldn't trust myself to walk in a straight line.

They sat there a while longer, but now they were alone they seemed to have nothing to say to each other.

Ruth decided she might as well bring up the Arrangement. Who could tell when she would see Dan again?

'By the way,' she murmured, keeping her voice cool and indifferent, 'your sister mentioned to me that she needed to go America to do some research for her latest book.'

Dan nodded, flicking a spot of ash from his pleated shirt-front.

'She asked if I'd be willing to look after Rosie and Danny for three weeks in August. You haven't mentioned it, so perhaps you've decided to make other arrangements for the children? I'm thinking of going abroad myself . . .' It wasn't true, but it sounded less pathetic than letting him know she was at a loose end.

Dan drew on his cigar and the tip glowed orange. He seemed in no hurry to give her a reply, even in the face of her direct question.

Ruth leaned her chin on her hand and pretended fascination with the engaged couple's royal progress among the diners.

'Can we discuss this later?' he said, at length.

Later? *When* later? Ruth gave a slow shrug of her bare shoulders and his eyes, following the sensuous movement, dwelled on the pearly sheen of her skin.

'Where were you thinking of going?' he asked abruptly.

'Oh,' she said, plucking a country from out of the air, 'Greece.'

'Now that's a coincidence——' said Dan rather smugly.

'Still here, you guys?' interrupted Edward. 'I've come to drag you away. Suzie's had this great idea.'

'Oh, come on, Ruth, don't be a spoilsport! You've got your bikini with you.'

Dancing with Dan had been wonderful, but short-lived. There were more women than men guests and many of them young and pretty; Dan was a smooth operator and in great demand. Never mind, thought Ruth, watching him strip off his jacket to dance with the confident little redhead who had hogged the front row in the jazz-dance exercise class. We'll be sure to get the last waltz together and they'll play a lovely smoochy number and I'll be in heaven.

Only Suzie had dragged them off, insisting on the four of them going for a midnight dip in the indoor pool. 'It's quite private. We lock the door, don't we, Edward? It's like a tropical paradise in there at night. We have the place to ourselves and we don't bother with clothes.'

Ruth dashed a hand through her hair. This was turning into a nightmare!

'Oh, *deàr*,' mocked Suzie, misinterpreting her sudden pallor, 'I never expected to see a nurse so shocked! You persuade her, Dan. Skinny-dipping in the dark is great fun.'

'It's no ordinary pool, Ruth,' put in Edward kindly. 'Palms and banana plants and discreet floodlighting. Quite a breathtaking effect at night. Suzie's teasing you, no skinny-dipping, I promise. OK then, Ruth?'

She nodded dumbly. What else could she do without seeming a total drip? In Suzie's bedroom she stepped out of her borrowed dress and her silken underwear and, feeling quite wretched, put on her pink strapless bikini and wrapped her shivering body in the big blue towel Suzie brought warm from the airing cupboard.

'Don't fret about spoiling your hair,' coaxed Suzie. 'I'll scrunch-dry you afterwards. With that good cut and your natural wave, you'll look good as new.'

'I ought to be getting back,' said Ruth vainly, through chattering teeth. That was rubbish and she knew it, but she was clutching at straws.

The men were already in the water, adept as sharks, heads wet-black as seals.

Suzie hadn't exaggerated. With uplighters the effect

was as of a tropical islet at dusk. Ruth would have been perfectly happy if only she could have just lain down on one of the luxurious sunbeds and watched the others frolicking fearlessly in the mysterious green water.

'Whoo-hoo!' Suzie threw off her robe and dived in, her body a white streak with two brief slashes of scarlet. The men converged on her and the place echoed with soft sound: water slapping, lapping, swirling, its surface heaving. Great palms and tropical ferns threw intricate shadows which formed dark secret places out of which the swimmers appeared and disappeared. Which was the shallow end? wondered Ruth in confusion. She dropped her towel and went gingerly to the top of the steps, too anxious to care about exposing her scantily clad body.

'Jump in!' cried Suzie joyously, flicking the long wet hair out of her eyes so that it whipped the air about her head, throwing out a hand to her.

'I—I . . .'

Edward dived between Suzie's legs and tipped her backward into the depths. Bubbles rose to the surface and the water boiled above their skirmishing bodies.

Ruth thought she was going to faint. She swayed on the top step, her hands gripping the rail.

Suddenly a dark shape reared up out of the water below and there was Dan, his hands reaching up to cover her wrists.

'I *know*,' he said urgently, and his eyes willed her to trust him.

He remembered what she had told him, about her father, about Jeff; he understood!

'Come down,' he ordered gently, his voice so calm

and reassuring that all hesitation left her, and she came down the steps and into the circle of his arms. 'I'm going to teach you,' he murmured, his lips caressing her ear, 'not to be afraid.'

Sighing, Ruth buried her head against his wet shoulder, feeling beneath her cheek the flexing of muscle and sinew as he raised his hand to stroke her head, his other arm firm about her body, pressing her close against him. Miracles could happen, and one was happening right now. She and Dan, the water striving to come between them, but quite excluded by the bonding of naked flesh. She didn't think anything would ever trouble her again . . .

Suzie switched off the hairdrier and ran her fingers through Ruth's springy curls. 'There you are,' she declared, 'dead easy. You see how it's done?'

'I don't know how to thank you. For *everything*. What a day it's been!' Ruth stretched ecstatically, then said, 'I'd better get a move on—I'm sure you and Edward want to be alone.'

Like Cinderella she had parted with her glamorous gown and was now wearing the strappy denim sun-dress she'd bought weeks ago in Bath.

'Do you want to borrow a sweater?'

'Oh, no, thanks.' I've got my love to keep me warm! Ruth hugged herself in secret delight.

'You girls decent?' enquired Edward, peering round Suzie's bedroom door.

Dan was waiting in Suzie's sitting-room. 'I'm taking Ruth home,' he said, in don't-argue-with-me-woman tones.

There was a wicked gleam in Suzie's eye. She and Edward had kept well clear of the love-birds smooching in the shallows. Things were working out even better than she'd hoped.

'We'll pick up Ruth's car tomorrow.'

'Splendid,' said Edward. 'See you both then.'

'I don't think I came this way,' observed Ruth doubtfully some ten minutes later. Ought the local GP to be seen driving and hugging her at the same time? Not that they'd passed any other cars at this early hour of the morning.

'I know exactly what I'm doing,' said Dan, planting a kiss on her sweet-smelling hair. 'Now if I can just have my arm back for a moment . . .'

The headlights illuminated a painted sign that said 'The Old Rectory'.

'Here we are,' said Dan, driving through wide-open gates and up to the front door of his home. A light shone to welcome them.

Ruth sat silent and uncertain, missing the comfort of Dan's broad shoulder. 'Are you sure you want me to come in?' she said uncertainly.

He was striding round the car to open her door. 'No,' he glowered, his voice rough with impatient desire for her, 'I'd much prefer you to sit here and freeze.'

She knew what he had brought her here for and was electrified. His hands reached for her and lifted her bodily from the car. Like being abducted! she thought crazily. She had no idea where she was—this big shadowy house surrounded by shadowy gardens and this big man handling her as if she belonged to him and he knew exactly what he planned to do with her!

Dan unlocked the door and reached to switch off the outside light. On the dark threshold, unable to contain himself any longer, he pulled her to him and proceeded to kiss her very thoroughly indeed. 'I was beginning to think,' he murmured against her ardent lips, 'that you and I were never going to make it.'

'Beatrice . . . Danny . . . Rosie!' gasped Ruth, sliding her hands under his open dress-shirt as simultaneously he undid the straps of her dress and pulled it down to her waist, kicking the door shut behind them.

'They're not here,' he groaned, dragging her towards the stairs. 'You and I are totally and completely alone.'

'Oh, Dan!' gasped Ruth. 'It's been so long. I'm not sure——'

'It's like riding a bicycle,' muttered Dan. 'I haven't forgotten how.'

It was midday before they woke, limbs entwined, to make love again.

For a long moment Ruth lay there believing herself deep in some wild, wanton dream. But the magnificent male body smothering hers was very real and totally demanding.

'Where is everyone?' she asked at length. Dan leaned over her, pinioning her with his elbow while the tips of his fingers explored the softness of her skin. 'Danny's . . . at computer camp. Rosie's . . .staying with one of her little pals. Bea's . . .living it up in . . . New Orleans. She's taken the vicar with her . . .'

Ruth sat up and the sheets fell away from her body. Dan rolled over on to his back, locking his hands behind his head, following her every move.

The bed was vast, the room beautifully furnished with antiques. Rosie's eyes—Ruth gave a start!—watched them from a large silver-framed colour photograph on the mahogany dressing-table. Only it wasn't Rosie but a lovely dark-haired woman in a yellow dress.

Ruth swung her legs out of bed and walked naked across the room to study these pictures of Dan's first wife. If he hadn't wanted her to look closer, he should not have brought her to this room.

He said nothing, his eyes intent, the lids heavy and watchful.

'Oh, Dan . . .'

He held out his arms and the gesture drew her back to his bed. He told her that he first met Juliette in Lyons where she was then studying archaeology at the university. He was working for six months at the city hospital. Within weeks they were married. He brought her back to England, but she never really settled. The marriage was not perfect; how many marriages were?

'What was she like?' asked Ruth.

'Eye-catching, chic. Quite different from any woman I'd ever known.' Thin, dark, volatile. Given, too late, he had discovered, to moods of depression and homesickness. He blamed himself. He should never have transplanted her from her native soil . . .

Ruth stayed with him that day. They both needed time to come to terms with the past and the sudden explosion of their long-simmering feelings for each other.

On Ruth's insistence, though, they collected her car and she drove herself back to Ditchingham House where she planned to spend that night alone. The weather had broken and rain teemed down from the leaden skies.

Just after eleven the bell rang at the main door.

'You're soaked to the skin!' she exclaimed.

Dan grinned ruefully, his black sweatshirt and denim jeans clinging to his powerful frame, his hair plastered to his skull. 'I've been walking round the grounds. I couldn't leave you.'

'Oh, Dan!'

He had a hot shower and while his things dried Ruth offered him her towelling robe. 'It's supposed to be unisex size,' she frowned when the thing proved far too small.

'I'm not your average man,' murmured Dan suggestively.

'You can say that again!' retorted Ruth, playfully flicking him with the towel she had fetched for him to hitch round his middle. They shared a very late makeshift supper and Ruth switched on two bars of the electric fire, snuggling up to him on her small Habitat couch. 'Isn't this romantic?' she sighed.

'Not very,' grunted Dan, biting her ear. 'I'm none too sure about your single bed. Shades of the Dragon watching over us.'

'*Don't!*' Ruth shuddered at the memories his remark conjured up.

'I've a very romantic proposition to make, though . . . no, don't sit up, let me tell you about it right here. Next week——'

'Mmm?'

'We shall fly to Athens, you and I, because you said

you were going to Greece and I thought I might invite myself along too.'

Ruth bit her lip with excitement at the prospect of a holiday, in Greece, with Dan Gather.

'Then we shall take a long ride on a big ferry to an island in the Cyclades——'

'Ah!' Ruth closed her eyes, picturing blue skies and wine-dark seas, white sugar-cube dwellings and hot gold sun.

'Where a good friend of mine named Savvas is right now smoothing the administrative details and organising our Greek island wedding in the sun.' Dan gave a stunned Ruth an extra-big hug. 'Any quarrel with that, my darling Silkey?'

She clapped both palms to her burning cheeks. 'My job! The school! Danny, Rosie . . .'

Firmly her hands were drawn away from her face and clasped within Dan's own. His voice was low and caressing and rich with love. 'You take your responsibilities very seriously, and that's one of the many admirable qualities in you that I deeply respect. But you can be replaced here in a way that you never can be replaced in my heart.'

There were tears in Ruth's eyes as she heard this. She was shaking her head, but she was saying yes, yes, yes . . . 'And Danny and Rosie must come with us,' she implored. 'Oh, *please*, Dan my dearest! We're going to be so happy together, the four of us. Let's start as we mean to go on.'

'I could never refuse you anything when you look at me like that,' whispered Dan tenderly. 'Your happiness is my happiness from now on. My children are your children, and soon there will be *our* children. I shall love and cherish and protect you for the rest of our life.'

Our life. Our future. The past fading into the past. Yes, sighed Ruth, if that's the prescription then I trust the doctor and take it.

SOLITAIRE – Lisa Gregory   £3.50

Emptiness and heartache lay behind the facade of Jennifer Taylor's glittering Hollywood career. Bitter betrayal had driven her to become a successful actress, but now at the top, where else could she go?

SWEET SUMMER HEAT – Katherine Burton   £2.99

Rebecca Whitney has a great future ahead of her until a sultry encounter with a former lover leaves her devastated...

THE LIGHT FANTASTIC – Peggy Nicholson   £2.99

In this debut novel, Peggy Nicholson focuses on her own profession... Award-winning author Tripp Wetherby's fear of flying could ruin the promotional tour for his latest blockbuster. Rennie Markell is employed to cure his phobia, whatever it takes!

These three new titles will be out in bookshops from February 1990.

W RLDWIDE

Available from Boots, Martins, John Menzies, W.H. Smith, Woolworths and other paperback stockists.

A Mother's Day Treat

This beautifully packaged set of 4 brand new Romances makes an ideal choice of Mother's Day gift.

BLUEBIRDS IN THE SPRING
Jeanne Allen
THE ONLY MAN
Rosemary Hammond
MUTUAL ATTRACTION
Margaret Mayo
RUNAWAY
Kate Walker

These top authors have been selected for their blend of styles, and with romance the key ingredient to all the storylines, what better way to treat your mother... or even yourself.

Available from February 1990.
Price £5.40

TASTY FOOD COMPETITION!

How would you like a years supply of Mills & Boon Romances ABSOLUTELY FREE? Well, you can win them! All you have to do is complete the word puzzle below and send it in to us by March. 31st. 1990. The first 5 correct entries picked out of the bag after that date will win **a years supply of Mills & Boon Romances** (*ten books every month - worth £162*) What could be easier?

```
H O L L A N D A I S E R
E Y E G G O W H A O H A
R S E E C L A I R U C T
B T K K A E T S I F I A
E E T I S M A L C F U T
U R C M T L H E E L Q O
G S I U T F O N O E D U
N H L S O T O N E F M I
I S R S O M A C W A A L
R I A E E T I R J A E L
E F G L L P T O T V R E
M O U S S E E O D O C P
```

CLAM	HOLLANDAISE	OYSTERS	SPICE
COD	JAM	PRAWN	STEAK
CREAM	LEEK	QUICHE	TART
ECLAIR	LEMON	RATATOUILLE	
EGG	MELON	RICE	
FISH	MERINGUE	RISOTTO	
GARLIC	MOUSSE	SALT	
HERB	MUSSELS	SOUFFLE	

PLEASE TURN OVER FOR DETAILS ON HOW TO ENTER

HOW TO ENTER

All the words listed overleaf, below the word puzzle, are hidden in the grid. You can find them by reading the letters forward, backwards, up or down, or diagonally. When you find a word, circle it or put a line through it, the remaining letters (which you can read from left to right, from the top of the puzzle through to the bottom) will ask a romantic question.

After you have filled in all the words, don't forget to fill in your name and address in the space provided and pop this page in an envelope (you don't need a stamp) and post it today. Hurry - competition ends March 31st 1990.

Mills & Boon Competition,
FREEPOST,
P.O. Box 236,
Croydon,
Surrey. CR9 9EL

Only one entry per household

Hidden Question _____

_____

Name _____

Address _____

_____

_____

_____ Postcode _____

You may be mailed with other offers as a result of this application.

mps
MAILING
PREFERENCE
SERVICE

COMP 8